The Scent of Bright Light

The Scent of Bright Light

Jean K. Dudek

RESOURCE *Publications* · Eugene, Oregon

THE SCENT OF BRIGHT LIGHT

Resource Publications
An Imprint of Wipf and Stock Publishers
199 W. 8th Ave., Suite 3
Eugene, OR 97401

www.wipfandstock.com

PAPERBACK ISBN: 979-8-3852-0045-0
HARDCOVER ISBN: 979-8-3852-0046-7
EBOOK ISBN: 979-8-3852-0047-4

VERSION NUMBER 01/22/24

Preface

THIS IS A WORK of fiction, although it is based on characters and events from the Bible, specifically Genesis chapters 12 through 23. Like most stories in the Bible, the story of Abraham, Sarah, and Hagar is lean; we are left to wonder about the details and about the characters' everyday lives. We could say that biblical stories leave a lot of blank spaces between the lines, between the words, and around the margins. My story fills in some of those spaces, reimagining the relationship between Sarah and Hagar in a way quite different from the traditional assumptions about it. The age-old plot becomes a new story when Sarah tells it.

The story of Sarah and Hagar comes from a patriarchal society. Patriarchy does not mean women never did anything or never had any power. But it does mean the bearers of the tradition (oral for a long time before written) were interested in men's concerns, not in what women did or wanted. Stories about women typically are told in terms of how they affect a man's story and reflect men's views of what women should be concerned about. Women are mentioned in terms of their relationship to fathers, husbands, or sons, not to other women. If there is interaction between two women, the interaction is typically about a man: rival wives, for example. (Two women pitted against each other. Who wins? The patriarchy.) It's easy to imagine a lot was happening in women's lives that the tradition-bearers weren't interested in or had no way of knowing.

I retold the story in Sarah's voice and gave Hagar an Egyptian name, Ta-Sherit. I imagined their relationship as something closer to, but not literally, mother and daughter—loving, but not without friction. Although mothers and daughters have existed since time immemorial, we can barely find a line of dialogue, let alone a relationship, between a mother and a daughter in the Bible. The closest is the story of Ruth's loyalty to her mother-in-law, Naomi. In another story, Miriam fetches her mother to be hired to nurse the baby found by Pharaoh's daughter, but that is as far as the mother/daughter interaction goes. Elsewhere, we can figure out that Maacah is Tamar's mother and Leah is Dina's, but these mothers do not even appear in the tragic stories of their daughters; the stories focus on the actions of David's sons and Jacob's sons, respectively.

Filling in the blank spaces and gaps in the text is part of an ancient tradition known as midrash. More casually, one could think of midrash as fan fiction. Some readers may compare it to the practice of "sanctified imagination" in Black preaching. Scholars believe that the stories in Genesis were told, retold, compiled, reshaped, and edited in view of later events. What was left on the cutting room floor, so to speak? What never even made it into the first telling? If the events I made up in this book had happened, would the keepers of the tradition have considered them important enough to remember?

A comment on language. Some readers might expect a biblical story to be told in "biblical language" and consider contemporary language to be anachronistic. The English language, however, did not exist during the Bronze Age, so technically, all English words are anachronistic to the period. Moreover, what "biblical language" should sound like depends on a person's preferred translation. For some, that is the King James Version. But I thought it absurd to have these characters speaking the English of 1611. Another popular translation, the New Living Translation, uses natural, everyday English, so some readers think that is how the Bible sounds. Other translations vary in terms of formality and vocabulary. Meanwhile, many people do not read the Bible at all and might be put off by language that others might consider to be appropriately "biblical." I chose to use contemporary English, including some slang. (And a touch of snark. If you can see Sarah rolling her eyes, good.) Although almost all the characters are uneducated, I did not restrict the vocabulary to simple words. It may be hard for us modern people to keep in mind, but "illiterate" does not mean "dull" or "incapable of complex thought." Sarah can't write, but she knows the power of words and she can talk, and now she is talking to you.

While writing this book, I thought about how Sarah and Abraham knew very little about God. It will be a long time before Moses and the law come along, let alone the rest of what we have in the Bible. Coming from a polytheistic background, what was their understanding of a god? They must have heard of gods who had not created the world, for example. And so, I made decisions about when to write "god" versus "God," something Sarah and Abraham never considered.

I also had to make choices about what to call God in this story. Identifying God's name in Genesis and Exodus is a rather complicated business, but this is not the time and place to explain the Documentary Hypothesis. I settled on "El Shaddai," which means, among other things, "God Almighty." In Exod 6:3, God tells Moses that God appeared to Abraham under that name. I decided to leave it at that.

Some readers may be familiar with the Gen 21:9 passage about Ishmael doing something that upset Sarah: Playing? Laughing? Mocking? There are reasons the verb is tricky to translate. The original Hebrew text uses a verb (which sounds like Isaac's name) but does not say playing with whom or what. When Gen 21:9 was translated from Hebrew into Greek, the translators specified "with her son Isaac." Some, but not all, English translations follow the Greek translation and name Isaac. I left Isaac out of this scene.

One of the Dead Sea Scrolls (1Q20, also called 1QapGen) comprises a manuscript of Genesis that adds material not found in the canonical text. It tells of Abram having a dream about a cedar tree (him) and a beautiful date palm tree (Sarai) that grow from one root. This dream leads Abram to conclude he should say Sarai is his sister, not his wife, in order to save his own life. I thought this tree image was charming (even if his interpretation of the dream was not), so I included this extra-biblical tale in the opening scene and used the tree metaphor throughout the text.

There's always a story behind the story. Perhaps my embellished version of the story will inspire you to read the original story with new eyes, think about it more deeply, and ponder the questions it raises. I hope this will be true no matter what your level of familiarity with the biblical text. I will note, however, that the better you know the Bible, the more allusions you will see to other biblical texts. But do not worry; there will not be a quiz.

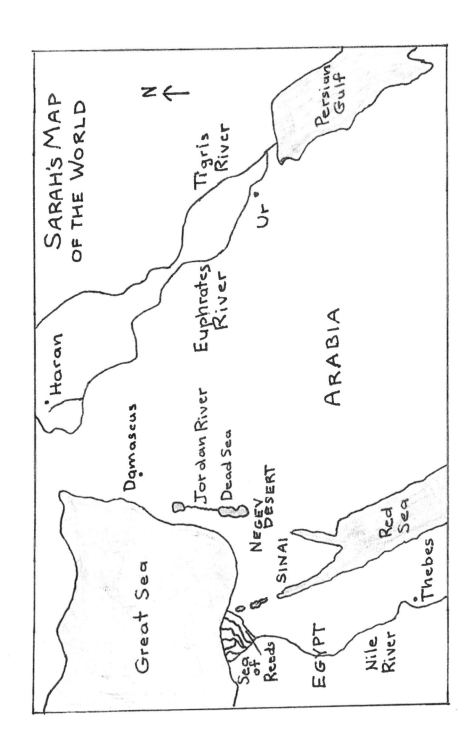

SARAH'S MAP OF THE WORLD

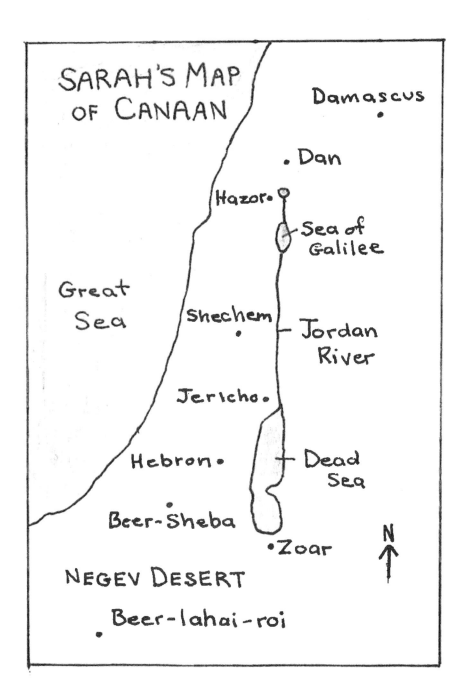

In and Out of Egypt

Chapter 1

I DIDN'T THINK IT was a good idea. "I don't want to do that! Why should I pretend I am your unmarried sister?"

"I don't think we have a choice," Abi said. "Here we are in Egypt; you know we had to leave Canaan because of the famine. We can always count on Egypt to have food. You want to eat, don't you? I'm going to tell Pharaoh's officials that you are my sister." He ordered me, "Play along if they ask you."

"But I am your wife!"

"Yes, Sarai, that's the point. If they decide to take you for Pharaoh and think you are unmarried, they won't need to kill me in order to make you available. Listen, it won't hurt for you to play along with this. They may never come for you."

But they did come, and Abi told his lie, and I told Abi's lie. I wound up trapped in Egypt, in Thebes, in the house of Pharaoh.

This "tell them you're my sister not my wife" idea started when Abi had a dream about a cedar tree and a date palm tree. He claimed he knew what it meant: we were supposed to pretend to be brother and sister, to protect him. Crazy. But I had no way out of this craziness. I could not escape from Pharaoh's house and even if I could get out of the palace complex, what could I do on my own? I don't know where my husband is.

It was true that the Egyptian officials noticed me when we entered the capital city of Thebes. That's not unusual. I am of pleasant shape and beautiful appearance, as they say. My radiant beauty is a blessing and the one special characteristic I have going for me. Unfortunately, this blessing does not cancel out the problem of my infertility, the problem I have been hoping to overcome all my married life. But all of a sudden, my beauty was a problem. It endangered my husband's life. Or at least, he thought so. Not that this had happened in any of the scores of other cities, city states, villages, kingdoms, or territories that we traveled through after leaving Haran. Or in our original home city of Ur.

And so, I was taken into Pharaoh's house and started my years-long captivity in his harem. Yes, it was the harem. Did you think I was there to bake bread?

It was a terribly frustrating time for me. All my life, I knew I was supposed to have Abram's child. It's hard to explain how I knew. Did the god who spoke to Abi tell me? And tell me in a way so that I forgot the telling but not the message? I don't know how I knew, but I did, and I knew it like I knew my own name. I'd known since childhood that I was going to be given to Abram and my sister Merai was going to be given to Og. That's the way we did it in Ur. You knew a long time in advance. I did not understand why my womb had been closed, and Abi and I constantly prayed that it would be opened. At first, we prayed to the gods we had grown up with in Ur. No results. Later, we prayed to the mysterious god who spoke to Abi in Haran. So far, no results. But Abi felt there was something powerful and different about this god, who had spoken to him personally, so we had hope.

I also knew that the purpose of my life was going to be about having Abram's children. In a way, every girl expected that her life would be about having and raising children, but I felt some mysterious sense of destiny about Abram and me and our baby. But there I was in Pharaoh's house, forced to have sex with him from time to time, which did not strike me as a particularly effective way to have Abram's child. Deeply frustrating. And disgusting.

Imprisoned in the harem, and not having to work all day every day, I had time to contemplate, or should I say, lament, how I'd gotten into such a wrong place. Was Abi's dream truly from our god? I didn't know if the god he and I refer to as El Shaddai has power in Egypt. The name El Shaddai means god almighty. When we heard from this god, the feeling was overwhelming. We were overpowered. We do not know the god's name, but the ordinary word for a god, El, alone, seems inadequate. All words for this god seem inadequate. And this god makes all other gods seem inadequate. Abi heard from this god for the first time in Haran and then both of us did in Shechem, in the land of Canaan. But I have not heard from our god in Egypt, and the Egyptians are very proud of the power of their gods. So, the dream may not be an authentic message from El Shaddai. Was it a message from one of the Egyptian gods, maybe an evil or trickster god? Or a demon? If so, it should not be accorded any weight. But I don't know.

I also wonder about the content of the dream. It was Abi's dream, not mine, so I can only know what he told me. "I dreamed of a cedar tree and a beautiful date palm tree," he explained. "Men came to chop down the cedar tree so the palm tree could be on its own. But the palm tree spoke up and said, 'Do not chop down the cedar; both of us have the same root.' And then the palm tree said, 'The one who chops down the cedar will be cursed.' Due to the palm tree's protection, the cedar was left standing."

But so what? And was there more to it than that? "The dream says nothing about you and me, Abi," I objected.

"I know how to interpret this dream," he insisted. "I am the cedar, and you are the palm tree. It was a very beautiful palm tree, Sarai. You must protect me from Pharaoh."

"Surely, if someone were to try to kill you, I would speak up to protect you. And do something, too, in addition to pronouncing a curse." I did not know what to make of the statement that we were both from the same root, although I liked that idea. "Does your dream say we should claim we are brother and sister? Doesn't the idea of our being from the same root mean that we should not be separated?" I argued.

No answer.

"Back in Haran, when you first heard from our god, you were instructed to leave that country, to leave your kindred, to leave your father's house. You were not told to leave your wife."

Again, no answer. I hope he knows what he's doing.

Chapter 2

BUT HE REFUSED TO listen to me. And we have been separated. Maybe this means the cedar and the palm will both die. Even if the dream did come from El Shaddai, Abi still could have misinterpreted it. It is hard for me to believe that my being trapped in the harem is what our god wants for us.

I have not seen Abi for a very long time. Is he still alive? If he is dead, I can't have his baby, that's for sure. I desperately wanted to get out of Pharaoh's house and return to my husband. But due to the guards, the record-keeping, the rules and the walls, it seemed impossible. And he may not be around anymore. What would I do without him and without a son? Life is tough for a woman without a male relative.

Only later would I find out that Abi's and my god sent plagues on Pharaoh's house to express displeasure and thus get me out of there. It took a long time, years, for Pharaoh and his extensive entourage of educated Egyptians to figure out there was a connection between those devastating plagues and the foreign beauty whom they thought was Abram's sister. At the time, all I knew was I was trapped and could not do what I knew I was supposed to do with my life.

I want to have Abi's baby and I can't.

Apart from this crushing sense of existential frustration, it was a dull life in the harem. Not much to do but talk with the other women. Abi and I knew a few Egyptian words from haggling with trader caravans passing through wherever we were living, and we picked up more of the Egyptian language during our journey to Thebes seeking food during the famine in Canaan. But since Egyptian is the common language of the harem, I was highly motivated to learn more. A strikingly beautiful young Egyptian woman and I gravitated to each other. She had the longest, flippiest eyelashes! She and I were the most beautiful women in the harem, although in different ways. She had beautiful, expressive eyes, and the traditional kohl eye makeup that we all wore emphasized them even more.

I have no complaints about the attractiveness of my own very dark brown eyes, but all my life I have particularly received attention for my excellent skin. Smooth, even-toned, never breaking out, never marred by any diseases. It's too bad it would be immodest for me to show more of it. But I know and Abi knows. And it's not just my skin. I have sleek, glossy black hair and my nails never break. People say that due to my perfect skin I radiate good health, and they predict that I will live a long time. I have also been told that I radiate dignity in the way I carry myself, and always have, even when I was a little girl.

"My proper name is Senbi," my new friend introduced herself, "but I've always gone by the nickname Bee-bee. Bee-Bee-Bay-Bee," she sang. Always up for a laugh, she didn't take herself too seriously, and neither did anyone else in the harem. I would not say that dignity was her strongest characteristic, but she was warm and willing to talk to me. Bee-bee had a lovely slender figure and a graceful way of moving. I wondered if the other women resented her for her beauty, and I wondered if they would react to me the same way.

She had some herbs she dried. Sometimes she chewed them and sometimes she smoked them. Either way, they were very relaxing. It was generous of her to share with me. She held up that little bag she kept them in and said, "Ya wanna?" with that big mischievous smile of hers. Little bag, big smile. I don't know how I would have gotten through that awful time without her. I've never found herbs like that again anywhere in our travels.

"My parents sold me to slave traders when our family fell on hard times and needed the money to buy food to feed my brother," she told me after we had become friends and were smoking her herbs together.

"I'm sorry that happened to your family. It's a terrible thing to have to sell a child."

"The slave traders—who I hope have died a horrible death by now—brought me to the attention of Pharaoh's officials. That's how I ended up here in the harem." She sighed. "I was a fabulously beautiful girl, everyone said so," she said, flipping those long eyelashes at me.

"Still are, Bee-bee Baby."

"I'm here now, and I have no place else to go. No point in dwelling on it. No point in dwelling on anything." She released a long, smoky exhale. "Smoke and vapor, smoke and vapor. It's all smoke and vapor."

Her live-it-up-today attitude kept her solidly in the present. She tried to avoid thinking about her past; I tried to avoid thinking about the sorry state of my future.

"You have to get through your days somehow," she mused.

I told her about my childhood with my sister. "Merai and I slept next to each other every night of my life until she was given away in marriage. It was a good year, a good harvest; people could afford things. Father gave her to Og and . . . " I was about to say, "me to Abram," but I caught myself. The official story was that Abram was my brother, and if it were known that he was my husband, both he and I could be in a lot of trouble. Trouble includes the possibility of Abi being put to death. So, I finished my sentence, "and I stayed home with our brother Abram."

"Nice to have that kind of prosperity."

"Merai and I used to talk at night, before falling asleep—planning, hoping, and fantasizing about what our lives would be like with our husbands, about the children we would have, about taking care of each other's children. I remember the first night of her wedding, the first night I did not sleep next to her. It was a hard night. We both had known, for a long time, it would have to happen sometime, but it was still a shock."

"Just like someone's death is a shock when it happens, even when you can see it coming a long time in advance." Bee-bee said this with a sigh that made me wonder how many losses she had encountered.

"I still miss Merai. She was the other one of me, at least until she was married."

"I don't miss anyone," Bee-bee said.

Og and Abram. I definitely had the better deal. I wonder if Father knew. My father and Abram's father, Terah, were good friends. It was no surprise that either Merai or I would be married to one of Terah's sons. I liked Terah and he liked me, so I think that's why I was given to Abram. Abram is a sweet man, calm and quiet. Some people think he spends too much time thinking. "He spends too much time in his own heart," a neighbor once said of him. I don't think that's such a bad thing. His heart is a nice place to be, so why shouldn't he spend time there? Another attractive feature of Abram is that he has perfectly formed bow-shaped lips. I don't know if there is a connection, but he is, in fact, a better-than-average archer. This is something that was never remembered and written down about him.

In contrast, Og was a brutal man. I'd heard he'd beaten a donkey to death. Og and Merai lived in Ur. I could still see her frequently when Abram and I lived there. After Abi and I moved to Haran with his father, Terah, once in a while we would get news of Merai when someone visited us when travelling from Ur. I would send a message to her along with anyone going back to Ur. I don't know if my words ever reached her. "It's been a long time since I heard from my sister. It is hard to imagine she is still alive. Despite how much I would like to think so."

So, I lounged on the cushions with Bee-bee, just like I did with Merai, at least, sometimes we did that when my sister and I both had a moment to rest. But these were Egyptian cushions, much finer than anything Merai and I ever had at home. Sometimes at night, I curled up, spoon style, with Bee-bee and fell asleep with her, just like I did with Merai, thinking about how terribly different my life had turned out from how it was supposed to be.

Another thing about Bee-bee: she had a lover. I know that sounds completely outrageous, seeing as she lived in Pharaoh's harem where the women are supposed to be exclusively for Pharaoh's use. They both could be killed for this. But those Egyptians, they were not so smart when it comes to guard duty. There were a lot more men than you'd think, both eunuchs and original-issue-equipped, in and out of our quarters.

One of the other women of the harem had a son who had grown up enough that he lived in another part of the palace. Sometimes he came to see his mother. One day a soldier, Hakkin, came with him. Hakkin looked around and naturally his eye fell on beautiful Bee-bee. Well, yes, me too, but I was older and wiser than Bee-bee and knew the value of giving a cold eye in certain situations. Bee-bee, always centered on the present and looking for a good time, looked right back at him through those beautiful eyelashes. So Hakkin used to sneak in and see Bee-bee. As a soldier in the Egyptian army, with no war going on just then, he didn't have much to do.

He was a jerk and awfully violent, even for a soldier. Always bragging about himself, bragging about who he had beaten up and who he was going to beat up next, making fun of his comrades, none of whom was as skilled or strong as he was, of course. I didn't like him, but there was someone else who truly couldn't stand him.

There was another lady in the harem, and yes, she was a lady, a princess from Punt or some such place. I don't know exactly where her father was the king; it seemed to be somewhere to the south. I've lived in a lot of places to the east and north of Egypt, but I'm a little hazy on the geography of the regions beyond Egypt in the other directions. I once tried to ask her about it and she just looked at me as if I were an idiot for not knowing. She had been married to Pharaoh as part of a treaty between Pharaoh and her father the king. I don't know what Pharaoh told him or what her father the king told her. But she had thought she was going to be much more important in the Egyptian royal hierarchy than she turned out to be. She was always aloof and putting on airs and mentioning her father the king whenever possible. From the first day I arrived, I could see that she was not pleased to be stuck in that harem with a couple of no-name beauty-dolls like me and Bee-bee. Not pleased at all. We called her "La Princezza." Unfortunately, poor La Princezza had crossed eyes and had either a speech impediment or maybe her voice just sounded funny because of the way her native language sounds. Hakkin-the-jerk used to do a hilarious imitation of her. I didn't like either one of them, but there was no point in letting them know that. Each of them annoyed the other much better than I could have, so I just sat back and watched the sniping. You take what amusements you can in the harem.

I've already alluded to what I was supposed to be doing in Pharaoh's house and that is what I did, and I did it well, whenever he called for me. Pharaoh was pleased, and pleasing the monarch is important if you are ruled by one. Beauty isn't everything, but it sure counts for something when a woman is stuck in a situation like that. You know that list of gifts he gave Abi? Sheep, oxen, male and female donkeys, male and female servants, camels. Well, think about it, it's not like Pharaoh of Egypt is going to give all those gifts, all at once, to some unknown immigrant herder from Canaan unless there is a good reason for him to want to reward that person. Bit by bit, time after time. You'll notice it's a fairly long list. And everything is plural. I don't want to go into too much detail, but I wish you could have seen the exact situation Pharaoh was in when he said, "I! am! going! to! give! your! brother! a! CAMEL!" We had not owned any camels prior to our sojourn in Egypt. I still kind of smirk every time I see one of ours.

One useful aspect of this unfortunate state of affairs was that if Pharaoh told me he was going to give my brother a gift, that meant Abi was still alive, and still in Egypt. These were the only clues I could obtain about my husband's situation. I was devastated to be separated from him.

Chapter 3

So, I WAS GETTING plenty of food and water, had no physical hardships, and was living in the house of a fertile man. What do you think happened next? Should be obvious, and yet, I couldn't believe it. I didn't know what to think. The whole point of my life was to become pregnant, and then I was pregnant and it was all wrong. I'd been unable to conceive a child all my married life, despite countless prayers, sacrifices and rituals. Why did god open my womb at such an inauspicious time? Was it an Egyptian god that opened it? I was dismayed that the baby would tie me to the house of Pharaoh for the rest of my life. If I ever did get out, I probably wouldn't be able to take Pharaoh's and my child, a prince of Egypt, with me. And if I could, what would Abi and I do with that child for the rest of our lives? The motivation for my going into the harem was to save Abi's life, not to have an Egyptian child. I wouldn't be able to leave the Egyptian harem part of my life behind and forget about it if I had Pharaoh's baby. And I desperately wanted to leave the Egyptian harem part of my life behind and forget about it. Worse yet, what if Abi rejected me because I was able to conceive, but had not done so with him? I couldn't stand the idea of Pharaoh's baby growing inside me when it was supposed to be Abi's child in my womb. I worried, what if the Egyptian baby contaminates it or ruins it or makes my womb Egyptian or something? Just like Pharaoh and his officials had ruined things for Abi and me.

And yet, I wondered if maybe I was supposed to have the Egyptian baby. It is hard to figure out what El Shaddai wants. Honestly, we did not and still do not know much about this god. We only ever received a couple of communications. In Haran, Abi had gotten the word that he was supposed to go to a land that this god would show him. The land turned out to be Canaan. It wasn't Egypt. Our god then repeated the promise of land

and descendants when we were in Canaan, at Shechem by Moreh's oaks. Life seemed to be going well for our household—with the major exception that I was still not getting pregnant—until the famine hit our area. Going to Egypt was the prudent course of action and we were not the only people from Canaan doing so. I had hoped once we were in Egypt and had plenty of food and water, I would be able to conceive. I certainly had not imagined I would conceive Pharaoh's child. Then, Abi had that weird dream about the two trees. I still don't know if it was a legitimate message from our god, but off to the harem I went. So maybe the pregnancy was supposed to happen. This god of ours is mysterious.

I wondered, I know I am supposed to have Abi's baby, maybe this is how? If it was supposed to happen in the usual way, why hadn't it happened yet? Not for want of trying, believe me. Maybe El Shaddai set this up as a way for something special to happen. Pharaoh would father the baby in the human way, but Abi would act as the father in some other, more important way of being a father? Abi could teach our child about El Shaddai, for one thing. Pharaoh could not do that because he does not know this god of ours.

But Pharaoh is not just a human; the Egyptians believe he is a god. Could I be impregnated by a god? There are ancient stories where that happens. Could someone be both a god and a man at the same time? Maybe Pharaoh is a relative of El Shaddai? Then it would be a child of god and of Abi?

Or maybe not. Pharaoh as a god? I don't think so. I've had sex with him. And I can assure you he is not a god. Not.

And another thing I wondered about: I had always thought that my womb was closed all those years with Abi, although I did not understand why. And then, when I was forced to have sex with another man, it was opened. I had heard about some infertile women whose husbands died and then the woman's womb was opened and she was able to conceive when she was with her second husband. Was Abi the infertile one, not me? That seems crazy, because men don't have wombs, so what is there to be closed or opened? Everyone knows infertility is the woman's fault. But it seems very strange that I am pregnant so quickly when I have not been praying and sacrificing for it. I have been in this body of mine for a long time, but I do not understand it. I wonder if I will understand it before I have to abandon it. We all have to abandon our bodies eventually and there's no reason to think an exception will be made in my case.

These were the thoughts that swirled around in my heart. I didn't understand what El Shaddai wanted. And even if I understood the plan, would I know what I was supposed to do about it? Sitting around in the harem, I had a lot of time to think about it. But I couldn't figure it out.

Bee-bee was smoking her herbs. Maybe I should just stop thinking and join her. Good ol' Bee-bee.

I hoped the baby would go away. I didn't tell anyone, not even Bee-bee.

Eventually, I had to face the fact that hoping does not make a baby go away, just as hoping does not make a baby come. I'd been hoping for a baby to come for a long time at that point in my life, so that part was perfectly clear to me. I had to do something more than sit around and hope the baby would go away. But what and how? Trapped in the harem, I did not have much control over what happened to me. That lack of control, in and of itself, infuriated me, and my anger strengthened my resolve to take action. I just had to figure out what that action would be.

The solution to my problem came from an unexpected source: Hakkin. I didn't like Hakkin, but fortunately, I had never made that known to him. He knew I was Bee-bee's best friend and trusted confidante. Hakkin apparently had the sense to develop some qualms about having an affair with a concubine of Pharaoh, and became concerned about the potential consequences if he got her pregnant. He had slipped me a bag of herbs that were known to cause miscarriage. "Bee-bee's kind of flighty, you know? So, I'm giving these to you to hang onto," Hakkin whispered to me confidentially. He wanted me to administer them to her if she became pregnant by him. "But if it's Pharaoh's, let it live."

I still had those herbs. Sorry, Hakkin, I never promised you anything.

I knew the herbs would cause contractions in my womb. I didn't know how strong and painful the contractions would be. I didn't know the herbs also would cause contractions at both ends of my digestive system. I didn't know what the appropriate dosage was, or how the herbs were to be prepared. So, I took the most direct route and ate the whole bagful at once.

I was sick for a week. There was so much blood. When the fetus came out, I wept, in pain and sadness and misery, even though I had accomplished what I was trying to do. It had eyes. Dead eyes that stared at me. And a mouth that looked as if it were laughing at me. A mess. A horrible nightmare of a mess. Even the afterbirth seemed to be taunting me.

I wrapped up the whole mess in an oiled linen cloth so the blood wouldn't soak through. At first, I was too weak to move, but I had to get rid of it. One day, I looked this way and that, and seeing no one, I sneaked outside. When a guard caught sight of me and questioned me, I said that I needed to go out to worship and sacrifice to a god. He accepted this flimsy made-up excuse and let me proceed. I hid it in the sand.

I lost a lot of blood and a lot of weight. I was deeply damaged. I was me, just me again, but I was so much less than I had been before.

Fortunately, Bee-bee came through for me. I am forever grateful. "I'm going to take care of you, Sarai," she said. "You must be sick from that nasty illness that's going around."

I think she knew that was not the case. But there were plagues beyond our walls that the Egyptian officials were concerned about. It was reasonable for people, both in the harem and among the officials, to conclude that I had come down with the latest illness. No one needed to know anything else, and fortunately, no one asked any questions.

"You need to drink; you need to eat; you need to sleep," she said matter-of-factly. And she knew something else that would help. Bee-bee had her herbs, her very relaxing herbs, so different from the herbs I'd just used. Bee-bee took care of me and got me through the physical part of my illness. Nothing got me through the emotional part except, perhaps, the passage of decades.

Once I was well enough to think about someone other than myself, I realized that Bee-bee had problems of her own. I spent a lot of time with her, and I was fairly certain she was pregnant. Just as it should not surprise anyone that my having sex with Pharaoh resulted in pregnancy, it should not surprise anyone that Bee-bee having sex with Hakkin resulted in the contingency he hoped to avoid.

"Bee-bee, I am right that . . . you know?" A significant look can convey a lot of meaning.

"Can you tell?"

"Uh, yeah, I have a special talent for knowing that. I don't think anyone else knows, yet."

"Stuff happens. Or doesn't happen, if you know what I mean."

"It doesn't matter if it's Hakkin's or his. Everyone will assume it's his."

"That's the problem. It's definitely Hakkin's child. Pharaoh hasn't called for me for a long time."

And that's the thing: these Egyptians kept records! If somebody thought to check, they would be able to figure it out. That would be serious trouble for Bee-bee.

Bee-bee kept her pregnancy secret from everyone but me for as long as she could. When Hakkin saw that she was pregnant, his eyes widened and he shot me an inquiring look. I met his eyes, gave him a tight little smile and shrugged. What could he accuse me of without getting himself into trouble? And despite his violent temper, he couldn't just haul off and assault one of Pharaoh's women. Of course, he wasn't even supposed to be in the harem in the first place. So, no repercussions for me.

Hakkin-the-jerk dumped Bee-bee when he found out. He would sneak in and flirt with some of the other women. He kept visiting the harem for a while, but eventually he stopped coming. We don't know what happened to him—maybe he went off to a battle or training exercise and he never came back from it. Or maybe he succumbed to one of those plagues. Or maybe he just lost interest. It's hard to remember when his last visit was, since we did not know it would be the last. I don't remember if he ever saw his baby or not. I think not.

Chapter 4

"SARAI, THIS IS MY first baby. I'm scared. I've barely even ever watched a birth. I can tell from things you've said that you know a lot about childbirth. Will you please be my midwife?"

"Of course, I will, Bee-bee Baby. I'd be more than happy to. I appreciate how you took care of me when I was sick."

There was a fancy set of birthing bricks in the harem for our use. These are children of Pharaoh that are born in the harem, after all. The birthing bricks were painted with pictures of Egyptian gods and goddesses and strange symbols that I suppose were intended to protect the mother and baby: a dwarf named Bes, a frog named Hequet, and, of course, the hideous hippopotamus-thing named Taweret. I don't know about all that decoration, but I have used birthing bricks countless times to support a mother and raise her, either crouching or kneeling, so that I could have better access to the baby.

It was a long, difficult delivery. Bee-bee kept screaming prayers to Taweret—the Egyptian goddess of childbirth—to help her. Most of the difficulties were typical, but one was not: the baby had the umbilical cord wrapped around her neck three times. It is not unusual for a cord to be wrapped around once; I'd dealt with that situation many times before, sometimes slipping it over the head, sometimes over the shoulder and down the body. No problem. Any midwife ought to be able to handle that. I had even successfully delivered some babies where the cord was wrapped around twice. I'd been present as a helper at a birth midwifed by another woman where it was wrapped twice, tightly, and she accidentally tore the umbilical cord trying to get it off. That was a bloody mess, and the baby did not survive. But I'd never seen one wrapped around the neck three times. The cord was the normal yellow color, but that was an unusually long umbilical cord Bee-bee had made.

Had to do it. Loosening it here, slipping one loop over the baby's head, getting some more play in the cord, another loop over and then at last down over her shoulder. Everything intact. Baby's neck was free, and she breathed. And I breathed and Bee-bee breathed. And Baby screamed the scream we all love to hear.

At last, after many hours of labor, Bee-bee had her baby, a beautiful girl. She was born with lots of thick, luscious hair and astonishingly long eyelashes, just like her mother. Bee-bee, unfortunately, had had a hard time, lost a lot of blood and was frighteningly weak. It would take a long time for her to recover.

"Is it a boy?"

"No, you have a beautiful little daughter."

"Oh." Her disappointment was palpable. She had hoped to increase her status with Pharaoh by presenting him with another son.

"Wait! There is something more! I have another! It's twins! This one will be a boy."

And out came the afterbirth.

"No, it's just the afterbirth."

"Is the afterbirth a boy?" She fell back from the birthing bricks and into the arms of the woman assisting me. She lost consciousness and we arranged her on her cushions and cleaned her up.

That is the weirdest thing I've ever heard a mother say after giving birth. I didn't think it was a good omen.

"That was the longest umbilical cord I have ever seen," I told her when she was conscious again.

"That means the baby will go far from me." She fell back into her cushions and fell asleep.

All of the women admired the beautiful baby girl, and even La Princezza unfroze enough to hold her and cuddle her. Everyone counted her tiny fingers and tinier toes, and admired her eyelashes. Bee-bee, with her typical disregard for preparing for the future, had not thought about a name. Pharaoh, or more specifically, he and his advisors, would have chosen the name if the child had been a boy or if the mother had been of high rank. Someone referred to the baby girl as Ta-Sherit-en-Senbi, which means Senbi the Younger, or more poetically, Little Daughter of Senbi. The rest of us eventually shortened it to "Ta-Sherit" and that became her name. She was popular among the ladies of the harem, so in a way she was the little daughter of us all, and Senbi didn't seem to mind her own name dropping off.

According to the records, I was supposed to have a baby, and Bee-bee was not supposed to have a baby. It's easy to see a solution to these problems. Those Egyptians are good at keeping records, but they are not so good at seeing what is actually going on. None of the women of the harem said anything, and I didn't know what any of them thought about the paternity of Bee-bee's baby. I noticed that no one referred to her as the little daughter of Pharaoh (or any of his various names, titles, or accolades) or little daughter of Hakkin, just little daughter of Senbi, uncontroversial and undeniable. Meanwhile, no one outside the harem cared about what happened in the harem. It's amazing the amount of silence that can be generated when you know no one is listening.

As far as the officials were concerned, the count was correct. Since it was a girl, it didn't matter a whole lot anyway. Bee-bee and I never had to lie. I happened to be holding Ta-Sherit and was playing with her on my lap when Pharaoh came in, and he quite naturally assumed I was the mother. We all breathed a sigh of relief, seeing that there were not going to be any questions. None of us wanted an investigation or for the rules to be any stricter.

Ta-Sherit, honey, you were a beautiful baby and every one of us women wanted to hold you and stroke you and cuddle you and play with you. Sweet girl with the long eyelashes! We all loved the smell of you. You had a lot of mommy-ing growing up in the harem, darling girl. You were blessed with physical beauty from your mother Senbi, with a regal bearing from La Princezza, with cleverness from another woman and with fortitude from yet another. During your early years in the harem, you were well-favored, but no one would have guessed how your life would turn out or what a blessing you would be for generations to come.

After delivering Ta-Sherit, I took care of Bee-bee, just as she had taken care of me. She was correct about me being an expert at delivering babies. Still am. That is something that was not remembered and written down about me. All my life I knew my goal was to have Abram's babies. I was always very focused on this. And for decades—as you well know, since my gynecologic status has been a matter of fascination for millennia—I did not have a baby. But it's not as though I just sat around being disappointed. "The weeping of a disappointed womb," that's what someone told me a long time ago about monthly blood. For better or worse, the phrase has always stuck with me. But I am more than a disappointed womb. I can hope and I can plan. If I wasn't doing, I could be learning. That was my way of fulfilling my mission: by becoming knowledgeable and prepared. So, I learned as much as I could about conception, pregnancy care, childbirth, breastfeeding, and infant care. I wanted to be the best mother ever. I wanted Abram to be proud of my ability as well as of my beauty.

Abi and I traveled a long way, through many lands. We started in Ur, we moved to Haran, then on through Canaan and to Egypt, bit by bit, stopping off countless places on the way. Not surprisingly, everywhere we went, some woman was having a baby. I learned about local practices in innumerable locations. I talked to as many women as I could about their customs, cures, tonics, incantations, exercises, and practices. I collected information, mentally cataloged it, and formed opinions on best practices when I acquired contradictory or bizarre recommendations—and oh! I have heard some mighty bizarre recommendations in my day. I worked hard at learning as much as I could and became encyclopedic in my knowledge.

I let go of collecting any more information about pregnancy and childbirth when I went into Pharaoh's harem, when it seemed hopeless that I would ever be able to use my information for the benefit of Abi's baby. But when my friend needed me for a difficult delivery, I was there, and I knew what to do. Returning to the role of a midwife seemed like the start of new hope. I mentally organized my information and recited it so I could remember it all. Then, I started to turn my recitation into a song, to sing my encyclopedia. Somehow, it is easier to remember a song than anything else. It gave my mind something to do, and my pregnancy and childbirth knowledge became quite a long song, an epic, even.

I taught Bee-bee how to care for her baby. Ta-Sherit was her first, and she did not know much about nursing or baby care. An amazing thing happened! I was able to breastfeed Ta-Sherit! Bee-bee was terribly sick and weak. She was unable to feed her baby at first and I was so desperate to care for that beautiful baby girl that I put her on my own breast. I felt a strange tingling and prickling I had never felt before but had heard about so many times. Ta-Sherit, of course, knew just what to do. Maybe somehow my own pregnancy, although terminated, made me able to have my milk come in when Ta-Sherit cried. I have never heard of such a thing. My body is more miraculous than I had imagined. This is such a special thing we mothers can do. There is nothing like it. I am grateful to Ta-Sherit for making me find out.

Chapter 5

THE BOREDOM CONTINUED. THERE wasn't much for us women of the harem to do. Pharaoh didn't call for someone every night, and there were quite a few of us. Sometimes we played a board game called "senet net hab." I'd never heard of it before, but it was popular among the Egyptians. It is sort of like the game of twenty squares that we had in Ur, but senet has thirty squares, three rows of ten. So that means you have to be able to count a little higher and I suppose that means the Egyptians think they are superior. Having enough leisure time to play a made-up game often enough to get good at it was an unprecedented luxury for me. The name "senet net hab" means "game of passing through" because a player moves their pieces from one end of the board to the other, but after playing many games of senet with some of the Egyptian women, I learned that "senet" also means "passing" in the sense of passing on to the afterlife. There were other Egyptian religious connections in the game that I didn't quite grasp and wasn't really all that interested in. How about focusing on getting something done in this life?

Egyptians are too absorbed with preparing for the afterlife. I never figured out what one does in the Egyptian afterlife. Keep on playing senet, maybe? What would be the point? If you are not Egyptian but you die in Egypt, are you subject to the rules and procedures of Egyptian afterlife? Apparently not all Egyptians get to the afterlife; that is why they put so much effort into preparation, to improve their chances. I did not want to die in Egypt. I did not want to enter the Egyptian afterlife, whatever it might be. I just wanted to get out of Pharaoh's house, get back to my husband and stop wasting time. Moving my pieces to the end of the board reminded me that I was not moving anywhere in this life, real life. But I did get good at this game.

Many of the ladies had looms and occupied themselves with weaving. I learned new weaving techniques from them. I didn't have my own loom, but there was one in our rooms that I could use. At least this let me feel like I was getting something done, even though I knew full well that it didn't matter. Our clothes (which were very nice, by the way) and blankets, cushion covers, and such were provided if we didn't make them ourselves, so we certainly weren't under any pressure to produce. We weren't exhausted from work at the end of the day, the way people usually are, and we had a lot of time on our hands. So, we talked.

There wasn't much happening in our little world, but occasionally we heard about palace intrigues or the plagues or what the officials were trying to do to counteract the plagues. Some of the women had children old enough to live "on the outside" and these adult children sometimes visited their mothers and told them the latest news. Most of the time, though, we told stories: stories of our past lives, stories from our homelands and about our gods (we came from quite a few different places), and stories that we made up ourselves.

I learned that the main god of Thebes was Amun. He is considered the king of the Egyptian gods and his name means "the hidden one." In paintings, he is colored blue, which is meant to indicate that he is invisible, as if he blends into the sky. But it seems to me that all gods are invisible, so what is so special about that? I felt like El Shaddai was especially invisible during this dull time of my captivity in the harem. Invisible and silent.

Then there is the goddess Mut, which is also the Egyptian word for "mother." She seems to be an all-purpose mother/creator kind of goddess. Some of the Egyptian women said Mut is Amun's wife, and others said she gave birth to the whole world through virgin birth. It seems to me that if she could do that, there would be no need for her to have a husband. She is often depicted with a vulture on her head. How attractive. A vulture on one's head does not strike me as a life-giving attribute.

Mut is, on the one hand, the mother of everything, and she is also, especially, the mother of the moon god, Khonsu. This family, Amun, Mut and Khonsu (Amun is the father of Khonsu, despite the virgin birth trick) is known as the Theban triad. What did any of these gods do for anyone, I wondered. Did they ever communicate with anyone the way El Shaddai communicated with Abi and me? If they did, would a person feel it the way we felt El Shaddai's presence? Abi and I both felt it in the same way. It's hard to explain, the way a dream is hard to explain, but you start to feel the presence of our god suddenly when you inhale. That means it's as simple as breathing and it happens as suddenly as an inhalation. And when it happens, the presence is as inevitable and unavoidable as breathing. You can't not breathe, just as you can't not feel the presence and power of this god when the presence is happening. The strangest thing about that inhale is that it smells like bright light. I know that light doesn't have any scent, but I can't explain it any better than that.

I just kind of nodded my way through these explanations of the Egyptian gods, although they did not make sense. None of these gods felt like a compelling figure. Stories of the other women's backgrounds were more comprehensible and therefore more interesting.

Bee-bee was only about twelve years old when her family sold her and she was taken into the harem. Her story began the way of so many sad stories: despite the famously reliable flooding of the Nile, there had been a bad year for crops. Locusts ate almost everything and there was little to eat and little to sell, but taxes still had to be paid.

"My father sold me to raise money to keep my brother alive," Bee-bee told me mournfully. "It was his decision, but my mother had suggested it. I was dismayed and felt betrayed. I had loved my parents. My brother did not love them more than I did. I had done no wrong. Yet this happened to me.

"Slave traders came through the area. They knew about the locusts and the economic situation and the pressure my family was under. They weighed out ten pieces of silver and off I went. Then, a small piece of good fortune: a grown-up woman slave they also held at that time determined that I was intact, and she told me to tell the traders that, while they might want to force themselves on me, they could get more money for me if they left me alone. Greed worked! Of course, their speculative greed did not make their other evil wishes go away, so some other woman was abused instead. Sometimes, it was the good woman who had advised me. She must have known this might happen. I am grateful for her sacrifice.

"We came here to the capital. I saw more people than I had ever imagined existed and so many things I had never seen before. I wonder if I will ever see them again. Pharaoh's soldiers stopped our group at the outskirts of the city. They had metal weapons I had never seen before. 'Any pretty girls for Pharaoh?' they asked the slave traders. They saw me. One of the traders said I was fifteen pieces of silver because I was intact. For a moment, I was outraged that they had only given my father ten when they knew I was worth fifteen. The soldiers said. 'We don't pay; we take.' For an instant I was outraged by that. But then I realized there was no point in caring about it. And they brought me here and that is that.

"But I do not care if my parents were cheated. I do not care if the traders were robbed. Being good does not matter. What matters is that I have food and water, and a safe place to sleep. Actions do not matter, and the gods do what they want. And so, my girlfriends, I say, look only to pleasure now. There is no point in planning for the future," Bee-bee concluded.

"One can plan to do things that will add pleasure or avoid pain," said another woman.

"Maybe once in a while there is a direct connection," shrugged Bee-bee. "But not often enough to bother with. The worst thing that happened to me, being sold into slavery so my family could get food during a famine, was due to nothing that I did. The best thing that happened to me, being beautiful enough to attract the eye of Pharaoh's soldiers and end up here, also was due to nothing that I did."

"You seem to have little use for the gods, Bee-bee. But where did everything come from? How do you think humans were created?"

"I don't know, and I don't need to know. My mother told me the story of Isis and Osiris. Maybe it's true. It doesn't matter if it is or not. The world is here, and we humans are here."

"That is not the story of my people," said another woman. "The people of Akkad say that Nintur, the mother goddess, created people out of clay and the blood of another god, We-ila, whom the other gods killed for this purpose."

"If We-ila was a god, how could they kill him?"

"They were gods, so they could."

"En-lil said to do it, so they could. Nintur didn't do it until En-lil said to."

"I was always told that her name was Belet-Ili, not Nintur."

"Belet-Ili is a title, not a name."

"Her name is Ninmah. That's what my people say."

"That's not it at all. Humans were created because of the Eye of Re. The eye cried tears that produced humans when Shu and Tefnut went to fetch it back."

"That's a silly story. How can a god's eye wander off?"

"Life is full of sadness. I think it makes sense that humans are made from tears."

"Tears from a god's eye. Humans are the sadness of a god."

"Not tears. Blood. Drops of blood fell on the earth, and a human sprang up from each drop of blood."

"Yes, that is the way it was, drops of blood falling on the earth. One drop becomes one person."

"You definitely need lots of drops of something. I once heard a story of creation of one man and one woman, but how can two people survive alone? You need a tribe, some kind of group, to survive."

"My father told me a story where creation was of one man, and all the people of the earth were descended from him. But that's ridiculous, as if the man can have babies by himself."

"Men wish they were able to have babies by themselves, without women."

"That would be fine with me."

"How can that be, the story about drops of blood falling on the ground to make humans? People bleed onto the ground all the time and more humans don't emerge from the bloodied ground."

"It must be special ground. The god would know and would say what ground the blood must fall on."

"It's very bad for menstrual blood to touch the ground. Never let that happen."

Then La Princezza spoke up, with her funny voice and authoritative attitude. "Stop squabbling. You are all telling the same story. The details are distorted in different ways in different places, but the same thread runs through them all. People came from the ground, in some way. We know seeds make plants in the earth. The first humans also came from the earth, but in a different way. So, what is the thing that is like a seed, to make the first humans? Drops of blood. It's a fast way for the gods to make a great many people, instead of a long pregnancy, and a long infancy, one at a time. The blood—I know what you're going to say—it has to be the blood of someone special, like one of those gods or demigods in the stories you are telling. That's why people don't form and spring out of the earth when blood is spilled on the ground. The name of the god isn't the important thing. Different peoples have given the same god different names. And the earth that it falls on, it must be special, like sacred ground. You know that soil has to be fertile for plants to grow in it. The gods know where the conditions are right. And it only happens when the great god says it should happen."

La Princezza was not particularly well-liked among us in the harem, but she was respected. Unlike the rest of us, she had some formal education.

She knew about plants, from trees to herbs, and about mammals, birds, reptiles, and fish. She was able to count higher than the rest of us. She knew about different cultures because she had listened to visiting ambassadors from other lands who had come to the court of her father the king. She was able to make analogies and draw conclusions. She was able to read and could write her name and some words in her own language—not that there is any opportunity for that in our rooms. In contrast, Bee-bee had trouble with numbers higher than ten. I once saw her take off her slippers when she had to figure out a number higher than ten.

La Princezza's explanation seemed to satisfy the group. Each of us could fit her own version of the story into La Princezza's pronouncement. And the basic story makes sense: the blood of a special person, a special area of land, the creation of many humans at once, and the say-so of a god.

So many gods, so many names. I wasn't about to try to tell them about my god. So far as Abi and I could tell, our god didn't have a name—or, at least, we had not been told a name—and was a god, or goddess, of everything, all gods in one, or one god above all others. We weren't really sure of that, but when we feel the power when this god communicates with us, we definitely feel something unique, unprecedented, a presence that is on a higher level. Something different from and beyond all the other gods and goddesses of this, that, and the other thing that we have ever heard of. Remember, we have travelled through many lands and heard about many deities, but no high god we had ever heard of seemed to be like ours. And no other god had ever spoken directly to us or to anyone we knew. That was the most important thing.

People want names for gods. They want an array of gods, each with a special characteristic or function. It helps a person feel in control: with a name and a function, you can put each god in a box. I don't know very much about this god of Abi's and mine, anyway, so I don't know what I would tell these women. Abi and I usually use the pronoun "he" when we speak of our god, but for no particular reason. We don't even know if this was a god or goddess; the voice we hear is not identifiable as masculine or feminine. Designating this god as male seems like a limitation on its powers and characteristics, and so does designating it as female. Figuring out the gender is the least of the mysteries we'd like to unravel. We think of our almighty god as El Shaddai, because the power feels stronger than anything we had ever imagined. It feels like a primordial power over all aspects of the heavens and earth. It would be a mistake to try to put our god in a box. We think of this

El Shaddai name as a placeholder, that there is some other name, or that this god is unnamable. Maybe we will find out later.

Knowing doesn't seem to be the point, anyway. It is more about feeling than about knowing: we feel that this god's power is such that Abi and I would do what was requested, whether it made sense or not. That the power would take care of us and make things right, somehow. But the god's power is not the whole story: the god seems to expect us to act, too. We could not just sit, like Abi's father Terah did in Haran, and wait for El Shaddai to make things happen. But we rarely know what El Shaddai wants us to do. I remember a proverb from when we lived in Ur: "A god's will cannot be understood; a god's way cannot be known; anything about a god is impossible to find out." The mystery of a god is never explained—whether mine and Abi's or La Princezza's. Maybe Abi and I will learn more about the character and intentions of El Shaddai. Maybe. I hope so.

Chapter 6

MEANWHILE, OUTSIDE OF THE harem, there was trouble: plague. Even though we were sequestered in the harem, we heard of the theories and debates about the origin of the plague, along with its effects. The son of one of the women visited his mother and gave us the news. "It started with the barley. Locusts came through and stripped the plants."

"Was any left?" asked his mother.

"A little. But what remains is of very poor quality, with small, shriveled heads," he said.

"I remember a locust plague when I was a girl, before I came here. That horrible rumbling, crackling noise of the horde as they came through! I was terrified," said Bee-bee.

"I've heard that noise, too. It's like the roar of an uncontrollable fire rushing through the land," said another woman.

"Lions roar and locust hordes roar. But locusts' teeth do more damage than a lion's teeth," intoned La Princezza. I wondered if that was a proverb from the land of her-father-the-king, wherever that was.

"What are the officials going to do?"

"The magicians, priests and advisors to Pharaoh started to investigate when it became clear the barley harvest in our area would be only a small fraction of a normal year's production. Naturally, their first line of inquiry was whether something was wrong with the little clay figurines of Osiris customarily planted with the barley during the annual inundation. Of course, the revival of the god Osiris and the revival of the land are linked," our informant explained.

"Oh, so that's how the Egyptian experts, or whatever they call themselves, deal with agricultural failure," I thought to myself. This Osiris theory was new to me. And unimpressive. Plenty of people in plenty of places grow barley without the use of little clay Osiris figurines. No point in my saying so, though.

"Our priests spent quite a bit of time on this theory. The displeasure of Osiris is the most likely explanation for a poor harvest when the level of the annual inundation is normal, as it has been this year. But they eventually determined that the clay Osiris figurines were the same as ever and placed the same way as usual."

"So, that isn't the problem?" asked his mother.

"No. Other possible causes have been proposed and are being investigated. It's gotten to be a big enough problem that they have suspended work on the Temple dedicated to Mut that they started to build over in Karnak. Some people say we cannot expend resources on it now, while others say attention to the gods is more important than ever during this time of trouble. It's a big controversy at court."

The next year, our visiting informant was back with more bad news. "More locusts came back for the wheat. Both the einkorn and the emmer types of wheat are afflicted."

"That's especially bad news, because no barley has been stored from last year," remarked La Princezza, who is better than most at remembering information and figuring out the consequences.

"It's been four kinds of locusts, now," said our visitor. "First, the cutting locusts. What they left behind, the swarming locusts ate. Then the hopping locusts ate what the swarming locusts left behind. Anything left by the hopping locusts was eaten by the destroying locusts." He used Egyptian terms for the four different kinds of locusts, so I wasn't sure what species he meant. But identifying the exact species was the least important aspect of his news.

"What about vegetables?" someone else asked.

"Thankfully, the locusts left the vegetables alone, for the most part, so some food is being produced. Beans, lentils, onions, garlic, radishes, they're all doing reasonably well."

"You can get along on that, assuming you have enough."

"What about ordinary grass?" I asked.

"Not affected. Grass is growing well. The locusts went for the heads of the barley and wheat."

This was a huge relief to me, as it meant Abi and his nephew Lot and the rest of our people would have grazing for our animals. Also, since the annual inundations had been normal, there should be plenty of water for the animals. The locust invasion did not affect the availability of water. I recognized that these locust invasions might work out well for Abi, if the decrease in grains causes people—at least, people who could afford it—to shift to eating more milk products and meat, which was what Abi was producing and selling.

"Do people outside the palace have enough to eat?" asked the mother.

"Some do, some don't. The poor people are eating locusts."

"Poor people can eat locusts," said La Princezza, looking directly at Bee-bee.

Yuck. I've been there. Not that I was going to say so there in the harem, but there have been times when I had to eat insects. I suppose there is some sort of rough justice: they eat your food; you eat them. But I have eaten only four kinds of insects: the ones we call locusts, katydids, crickets, and grasshoppers. I hope I will never have to eat them or any other kind of insect again. I imagine you could get used to it if you had to, but really, yuck. Fortunately, it did not come to that for us in the palace. And I hoped it had not come to that for Abi and our household.

On a more pleasant note, I was aware of the relationship between increased demand and increased price. If Abi was selling meat, he could be doing quite well. He would have to figure out the best proportion of how many animals to sell for slaughter versus how many to keep for further breeding, but he had been through other locust invasions and famines. He and his long-time chief steward, Damascan Eliezer, know what they're doing.

But all of that assumed that Abi and our household were still in Egypt. We came to Egypt to flee a famine in Canaan. Then Egypt, or at least the area around Thebes, started having plagues of locusts that caused food shortages. I couldn't get any information on conditions in Canaan, an unimportant hinterland as far as the fine people of Thebes are concerned. Could Abi have gone back? And left me here? I have not heard from El Shaddai the whole time I have been in the house of Pharaoh. Could El Shaddai have told Abi to go back? Without me? Would Abi do that? Yes. If El Shaddai told him to, yes, he would. I didn't want to think about that possibility. This whole relationship with El Shaddai started with a command to Abi to leave his father and family.

Pharaoh had not said anything about Abi for a while, but that didn't prove anything. And of course, there was always the possibility that Abi had died. I didn't want to think about that, either. Wouldn't I have felt it if he had? After all, we are both from the same root.

In addition to the plagues of locusts, Thebes was undergoing a series of plagues of illnesses. Some people thought the illnesses were because people were weak due to starvation. But the illnesses seemed to be contagious, and starvation is not contagious. There were endless debates about the illnesses, their cause, and their treatment. Waves of illnesses, with different symptoms, came through like the waves of locusts. Being part of the palace complex, we women of the harem were insulated from the food shortages, and since we were kept apart from most people, we were spared the worst of the contagious illnesses. As it turned out, I was lucky there was some illness in the palace, because it served as a cover for my own period of, shall we say, self-induced malady. But even so, Egypt was supposed to be such a great place. Instead, there had been nothing but one trouble after another in Thebes ever since I arrived.

Yes, nothing but trouble *ever since I arrived.* I had no idea there was a cause-and-effect relationship. Our household had spent days traveling along the eastern shore of the Nile through Egypt to get to Thebes—we'd even gotten a glimpse of the old Pyramids of Giza west of the Nile—and the land seemed to be prosperous and fertile, unlike the famine-stricken area of Canaan we had left behind. You had to go to Thebes, the capital, to ask Pharaoh's officials for food. That's where Abi had the dream about the two trees and came up with the "tell them you're my sister" idea that landed me in the luxurious wasteland they call the harem.

It took years for Pharaoh's magicians, seers, priests, officials, and record keepers (and they keep a lot of records in Egypt) to figure it out. After they determined that it was not a problem with the little clay Osiris figurines, they took out their elaborate silver and gold divination cups and worked through a great number of other theories as to why one of their many, many gods might be offended. Proposals for how to propitiate said offended gods took a while to implement, and guess what: none of them worked.

Meanwhile, the exact nature of the trouble kept changing. First, locusts ate the barley, then that variety of locusts died and they stank. Then a bird disease. Then swarms of a different type of locust came through and damaged the wheat crop. Then a die-off of fish in the Nile. That really stank. Human illnesses also appeared and disappeared and re-appeared. The magicians, advisors, and seers were constantly trying to figure out the cause of each new calamity. After a few years of this, someone, somehow, had a breakthrough revelation and determined that the source of the problem was in the house of Pharaoh. All the plagues were limited to the area around Thebes. Even when the source of the problem was pinpointed to the house of Pharaoh, there were plenty of people to blame, plenty of theories, leading to finger-pointing, accusations, conspiracies, betrayals, and backstabbing. Oh, the joys of life at a royal court!

At first, we women of the harem were ourselves insulated from the swirling controversies, but some of the women had sons who were grown-up enough to be at court. They kept up with, propounded, or were themselves the subject of, the latest theory of causation. They were also our primary source of information about what was going on outside our walls.

As part of the royal household, we always had enough to eat and good water and beer. Supplies could be brought in from the provinces; Pharaoh can take what he wants. The types of food we were provided changed from time to time, as different plagues affected different crops and animals. I was relieved that lamb, goat, and beef were on the menu in steady rotation, which suggested that those kinds of animals were surviving well enough and that herds and flocks, hopefully including Abi's herds and flocks, were healthy and able to find food. Maybe this sojourn in the harem was our god's way of keeping me fed and healthy during these cascading plagues and food shortages. I just hoped Abi and company were doing well, too.

But I said "hope." I did not pray. I did not sacrifice to our god. I could not feel our god's presence in the harem. I recalled the last time I did hear from El-Shaddai, way back in Shechem, and it seemed like a long, long time past. It was so long ago it crossed my mind to wonder whether it had really happened. Yes. It did. The experience was too overpowering to be questioned. You don't get hit by lightning and then wonder if it really happened.

Eventually, the suspected origin of the troubles was narrowed down to the harem—I have no idea how the diviners came to that conclusion—and each of us women was under scrutiny. The officials have records of when each of us was brought into the harem. They had already investigated my arrival date, but it did not correlate with the start of any of the plagues—for which they had detailed records, so there were plenty of dates to compare. More time passed.

Eventually, Pharaoh's record keepers figured out that the plagues started when I first was called for by Pharaoh. Although they had previously checked my arrival date, they eventually remembered that the protocol in the harem required that I not go to Pharaoh for at least two months after my arrival, to ensure I was clean, not sick with anything contagious, and not already pregnant. (Hah!) They had a record of my first visit to him, because they kept records of oh so many things, and it took them a while—years, in fact—to think of that criterion and to check it. But then, they knew. My initial disgrace (oh, why mince words: the first time Pharaoh raped me) and the arrival of the first swarm of barley-eating locusts coincided exactly.

Once they determined I had something to do with the source of the problem, they could have just killed me and hoped that would propitiate the offended god and make the problem go away. But fortunately for me, someone told someone who told someone who told Pharaoh that I am the wife of Abram, not his sister, at which point it was clear that the reason for the divine anger causing the plagues was Pharaoh's taking of another man's wife. Nice to know that the Egyptians assume that their gods have some standards of morality. I didn't know about any of this at the time, of course. I only found out later by listening to the guards hustling us out of Egypt.

Chapter 7

AND THEN, ALL OF a sudden, the big day arrived, and it arrived without warning. Pharaoh brought Abi into the women's rooms with him, angrily demanding, "What is this you have done to me? Why didn't you tell me that she was your wife? Why did you say, 'She is my sister,' so that I took her for my wife?"

Pharaoh was indignant. Abi was embarrassed. I was ecstatic. I was never so thrilled to see anyone as I was to see my Abi. My anger at him for putting me in that horrible situation had risen and fallen over the years: I had come to recognize that anger would not get me out of there. My surprise at seeing him turned into overwhelming joy when I realized what was happening. I was getting out and going with my husband! "Your wife. Take her. Be gone." Yes, yes, and yes!

Pharaoh told me to gather my belongings and that did not take me long. I had come in with very little. Pharaoh had given me some gifts. I had fine Egyptian linen clothes, but nothing left from what I'd been wearing when I was taken. I had woven a few items for myself during my captivity. I had a half-finished blanket, very fine wool with the beginning of a complicated pattern, on a loom. The loom wasn't mine and I certainly wasn't going to try to have the loom disassembled so I could take it with me. I cut the blanket off the loom, just the way it was, an odd size, unfinished and with the pattern asymmetrical because it was incomplete. I have treasured that little blanket ever since as a reminder that the unexpected can happen—and can happen fast.

Abi had no answer to Pharaoh's questions and was silent. No words coming out of the perfectly formed bow-shaped lips that I would soon be able to kiss again. Trying to explain the fear he had felt years ago when we entered Egypt would not only sound weak and stupid, but would also involve impugning the integrity of Pharaoh's officials, which is not a great idea for anyone in Egypt, especially a foreigner. I recalled what the beautiful palm tree had threatened in Abi's dream: "cursed will be the one who . . . " Pharaoh had been cursed even though no one chopped down the cedar tree. And now, the cedar tree and the palm tree that had the same root were reunited, and that root would be removed from Egyptian soil.

We stood before Pharaoh. Despite his anger, he seemed to want to give us a blessing and for Abi to give him a blessing. But neither of them knew what to say. Pharaoh caught sight of Ta-Sherit, took her by the hand and put her hand in mine. "She's your girl?" He said it as both a question and a statement, and he used a word for "girl" that can mean a female child or a female slave.

I caught sight of Bee-bee who was standing beyond Pharaoh, where he couldn't see her, her beautiful eyes flaring, and motioning that I should take her. Shocked that she would give away her daughter, my jaw fell open. But my dismay wasn't going to make me object: at last, I could leave with my husband and that was what mattered. I snapped my mouth shut and clasped Ta-Sherit's hand. "Yes, my lord. My girl." All those years of wanting a child, and this is how I got one.

Abi assumed she was a servant girl in the harem and that she was one more gift of a slave. Pharaoh had given him many male and female slaves during this sojourn in Egypt, after all, so why not another one as a goodbye present?

As for Pharaoh, he may have thought that I was her mother. That might be what the records said, if he ever thought to consult the records. And maybe he wanted to give me a gift of the one whom he thought was our daughter, as a kind of blessing. He didn't need any extra daughters. Those plagues had been damaging his household and kingdom for years, and once he had identified the long-sought explanation of their cause, he wanted Abi, me, and everything associated with us out of his kingdom. And he wanted the farewell to be done completely and properly, whatever that might mean for an Egyptian.

Bee-bee had been growing increasingly uncomfortable about Ta-Sherit as her features were developing so that she did not look like Pharaoh, but instead, like Hakkin. Pharaoh did not have the beautifully shaped nose Hakkin had bequeathed to Ta-Sherit. Fortunately, Ta-Sherit did have her mother's big, beautiful eyes and long, thick eyelashes, and she was a fine, graceful child. Although I am reluctant to say anything good about Hakkin,

I have to admit he was not bad-looking. It wasn't usually in Bee-bee's nature to worry, but she was worried about the child's likeness to her father. Having little experience with the emotion, she reacted by getting rid of the source of the worry in the quickest, bluntest way. Strategic thinking was not Bee-bee's long suit, but she solved the problem.

If Bee-bee were to be found out—and that could happen since a number of people knew about Hakkin—Bee-bee would be killed. I suppose Ta-Sherit would be thrown out on the streets. Or maybe handed off to slave traders. I don't think she would have lasted long on the streets. Starvation? Being eaten by wild dogs or jackals? These things happen. Or maybe Pharaoh's officials would have her killed, too. No royal Egyptian mummification and funeral for this child of the harem.

Doesn't matter. None of that would happen. Ta-Sherit was with me, and we were out of there.

An Egyptian soldier sullenly escorted the three of us to Abi's encampment, with my bundles and chest of personal possessions, together with Ta-Sherit's clothes, loaded on Abi's donkey. I noticed that Abi had a new walking staff, made of good strong Egyptian acacia wood. The old one was oak, made from a branch of one of the oaks of Moreh at Shechem. Whenever I had thought of him, that oak staff was part of my mental image. I wondered what had happened to it, but no matter. Surely, I should have expected that things would change. And in fact, things at our camp had changed. I was surprised at how many tents there were, how many cooking fires. Women I didn't know were cooking, carrying water jars, carrying firewood. The soldier announced that everyone was to pack up and leave the next morning to go back to the land of Canaan. He'd seen how angry Pharaoh had been, and he clearly didn't think much of this bunch of dirty herders from Canaan.

Lot and Damascan Eliezer greeted us on our return—oh, it was so good to see their familiar faces again!—and made plans for moving the herds and packing the camp. Lot suggested selling as many animals as possible that day so as to have fewer to care for on the journey. Eliezer knew that the plagues had primarily affected the wheat and barley only in the area around Thebes, and therefore we should be able to obtain food as we traveled north along the Nile. As the camp transformed into a whirl of activity packing up to leave Egypt, I scooped up Ta-Sherit and held her on my hip. She rested her beautifully shaped head with its long silky sidelock against my neck and she took it all in, surveying this strange new world calmly, from the safety of my arms. "I still have you, Mama Sa-Sa," she said quietly.

Chapter 8

THE FIRST EVENING, WHEN I told Abi I wanted to take an animal to sacrifice as a thank offering to El Shaddai, he said he wanted to do the same. Sweet Abi. "I am so blessed to have you for my wife," he murmured. "Rarely are great beauty and virtue combined in one person they way they are in you."

When he took me out to the flocks to select our sacrificial animals, I was astounded by how many animals he had. I was also surprised that I had forgotten what a large group of animals smells like. Our rooms in the harem were always nicely scented with Egyptian incense. My husband's situation had changed drastically due to his accumulation of wealth in Egypt. Pharaoh had given him a great deal of livestock because of me. Abi had done well with it, prospering while others had been afflicted with plagues.

But I noticed one animal was missing: Abi's favorite dog. "Where's Beezer?" I asked.

"Poor old Beezer died two years ago," he sighed.

We both loved that dog. "Noble beast," was all I could think of to say.

After a sigh and a pause, Abi continued. "Remember the first time I heard from our god? In Haran, telling me to go to another land?"

"Of course."

"I never told anyone this before, but I honestly believe Beezer heard the voice, too. She was with me when it happened. Or at least, she knew something unusual was happening. She stood still, quivering, with an odd look in her eyes. I felt even more closely bonded with her after that. It was hard to lose her." Pulling himself back together, he said, "Dogs have shorter lifespans than we do. Enduring their death is part of owning a dog."

All those times I'd worried if Abi had died, yet it had never occurred to me that Beezer might die. I recognized there would be changes in our household while I was trapped in the house of Pharaoh, but some were more foreseeable than others. It is said that people fear change. I think it's really that people fear loss. No one is afraid of a change like the increase in wealth that had obviously come to our household. I certainly wasn't afraid of the change of finally being set free and going back to my husband. But good old Beezer's death truly was a loss. My joy at my reunion with Abi included a little sadness at the edges.

Abi and I made our offerings and I felt cleansed, released, and ready to resume my life. Abi and I were together again and I was optimistic that our god would be with us. I felt like I could pray again. Praise god from whom all blessings flow.

The first evening of our release from the harem, after Abi and I had made our thank offerings, I took Ta-Sherit with me to an open area beyond the edge of the camp. The night sky was an amazement to Ta-Sherit. Upwind of the animals, the air smelled sharply fresh, and the sky was clear. The moon was amazingly beautiful. It was just past the new moon, and it was the thinnest crescent imaginable, sharp and bright, yet so slender as to be just barely visible. Ta-Sherit had never seen the moon like that. She was mesmerized by its beauty and unexpected, inexplicable shape.

"This night is different from all the other nights of my life," she said.

"Some nights are like that," I answered happily.

It had been a long time since I had seen the moon, either. It made me feel as though I was back on track for doing what I was meant to do with my life, and that brought me great joy. The moon is how we keep track of these things, after all. It was a waxing crescent and I felt hopeful knowing it would get bigger and bigger. Please, please, please let me get bigger and bigger, too. And who knew where we would be when the next new moon came? The Egyptians believe that the crescent moon was when women were fertile. I knew that was not true, but I took it as a sign to be hopeful.

The next morning, we were up early, as everything had to be packed up as quickly as possible. Tents, tent poles, ropes. Put the tent pegs and hammers someplace where you can find them when setting up again at the end of the day. Clay ovens. Looms. Sleeping mats, blankets. Grindstones, jars of oil, jars of water, oil lamps. Sacks of grain, sacks of hops. Fortunately, we had more ox carts and the oxen to pull them than we did when we arrived in Egypt.

The second night, Ta-Sherit, excited, tugged on my arm begging to go out to look at the moon again. "The moon moves across the sky. It rises and sets like the sun does," I told her.

"Really? The moon does that? I only knew that Re travels across the sky each day."

"Unlike the sun, the moon changes shape. It will grow ever so slightly bigger and bigger each night until it is a completely round disk. From one night to the next, you can barely tell the difference, but in fourteen days the shape will be fully round. Then it will get smaller, again in barely noticeable stages, until it is gone."

"Why does it change shape?"

"I don't know. There are stories, but I don't think anyone knows for sure. I can tell you that the moon's rising and setting is different from how the sun does it. When the moon is a tiny crescent like it is tonight, it rises with the sun and sets with the sun. But when it is a full round moon, it rises at sunset and sets at sunrise." She has hardly ever been outdoors, I thought. She has so much to learn.

"I remember seeing a statuette of the moon god—what is his name? Khonsu—with both a crescent and a full disk on his head. Mama Bee-bee told me that Khonsu was used to mark time. But I did not know what that meant, since all days seemed the same to me. How do we worship Khonsu? Mama Bee-bee did not tell me what to do to worship."

So much to learn and so much to unlearn. "We don't worship the moon. My husband and I worship a different god. You really don't need a god for this, that, and the other thing. When our god speaks to us, we feel like our god saturates all the world, all that is. And that includes the moon and the sun. So, our god is bigger and more powerful than the sun or the moon, or anything else. And this god should saturate your imagination, too, Ta-Sherit. This god has now freed me from the harem and I can exit Egypt. I am out of the house of Pharaoh and now am where I belong, in the house of Abram." I hope she will notice my joy for what my god has done for me.

"Will there be a house? Tonight, we are sleeping in a tent. I am Egyptian. Will I stop being Egyptian if I am not in Egypt? My father Pharaoh is descended from Re. Does that make me a descendant of the sun god, too?"

"We will talk about these things later, Ta-Sherit. Right now, just look at the sky."

As we traveled out of Egypt, our group was in some ways protected and in some ways treated like prisoners. I overheard an official repeating Pharaoh's orders to the soldiers who would accompany us. "Pharaoh wants these Canaanites or Amorites or whatever they are out of here, fast.

All these people and their animals and their belongings, all that this man Abram has. Do not let anyone disturb or delay them on their trip out of Egypt. Keep them moving every day, straight through, no stopping except at night. Get them to the other side of the Sea of Reeds."

Abi was a rich old man without a son to be his heir. Lot, the son of his deceased brother Haran, would be the obvious choice, wouldn't he? Another possibility was our servant, Damascan Eliezer. He was an excellent manager who had been with Abi for a long time. He was a servant who had been born in our house, and Abi trusted him fully. I knew I had better have a good relationship with whichever one of them turned out to be the heir if Abi died before me and I did not have a son. I was in a fortunate situation at that time, but I was well aware that sudden-onset poverty was a real possibility for my future.

I thanked our god that I was with Abi again. He had always been the great love of my life, despite my rage when I was first taken into the harem and my dismay over how my husband had used me. My disgrace was over at last. I thought of Bee-bee's focus on the present. It's over now, I kept telling myself, and now I will get back to what I was meant to do. Move forward and do not look back. I love Abi and love does not keep records of being wronged.

Abi and I barely talked about what had happened in the intervening years. We had no privacy with the guards and soldiers around us, so we both felt too intimidated to talk much. Moreover, the sudden increase in physical activity due to the orders to keep moving had us worn out by sundown. Abi told me what I needed to know for practical reasons. By the time the soldiers left us, and we could speak more freely, we'd shared the major news. Neither of us had heard from our god during our separation. There did not seem to be any point in telling him about my life in the harem, and I didn't want to risk stirring up my old anger.

It took me a few days before I stopped wearing my Egyptian wig. It was a great big black thing that pushed my ears forward so that they stuck out. All upper-class Egyptian women wore them, and the wig had been made for me when I entered the harem. I got used to it; one can get used to almost anything. Travelling in the sun all day, it felt hot and heavy. Wigs like that were not the custom among our people. Maybe it made me look more authoritative, but it also made me look like a foreigner among my own people. I didn't feel the need to impress the Egyptian soldiers accompanying us. They knew what my story and my status were. I wondered how long it would take for my ears to lie flat against the side of my head again.

I stopped making up my eyes with kohl. Not a lot of time to apply it when we were on the move starting early every morning, and just not a lot of point in doing so. I had a nice cosmetics box, lovely inlaid woods, beautifully joined, which wound up at the bottom of my bag of personal possessions since it was not being used any more. My ivory spindles also made their way down to the bottom of the bag due to lack of use. No time for spinning while moving out, but I looked forward to being able to use them again once we settled down in Canaan. I liked the feel of them in my hand—it's so gratifying to use a practical item made of a luxurious material.

I felt more and more natural, more and more like myself, as we journeyed north towards Canaan, as I dropped one Egyptian habit after another. One habit I kept, however, was that of wearing linen shifts. They are lighter and more comfortable against the skin than the traditional woolen clothes we wear in Canaan. At that point, the linen clothes were nearly all I had. Abi had saved my second-best shawl, and I was happy to see it again. "It smelled like you for a while, but after all these years, I must admit it smells like me," he laughed when he presented it to me on our first night. I suppose the Egyptians burned the clothes I was wearing when I entered the harem. They pay much more attention to bodily cleanliness in Egypt than we do in Canaan or Haran or Ur. Since we were travelling along the Nile, I had access to water for washing, but I knew that my frequency of bathing was going to decrease once we turned northeast away from the Nile.

There were some pleasant aspects of that long journey along the Nile. On the way to Thebes so many years ago, fleeing the famine in Canaan, we were worried and hungry. In contrast, on the return trip north, we had enough to eat and of course plenty of water from the river. I can't say that we became friends with the Egyptian soldiers, but as time passed, we came to realize that they were not going to harass or harm us. I could only guess what they had heard about our god and/or the reason for the plagues, but the soldiers may have felt cautious about offending this rag-tag group of herders who seemed to have a powerful god looking out for them. Meanwhile, the presence of Egyptian soldiers greatly decreased the chances of our being attacked by raiders, bandits, wild animals, and wild chieftains.

It is possible to transport animals by boat on the Nile, but our herds and flocks were so numerous that doing so would have required a huge flotilla. Pharaoh was not going to provide such extensive resources, even if he did want us out of Egypt, so we walked. I have to admit that some of the scenery along the Nile was beautiful. After so many years of being cooped up indoors almost all the time, it was delightful to see sunshine glinting on the water, and southbound wooden boats gliding by with their wide rectangular sails catching the wind. I figured out that the current flows north, but the prevailing winds blow to the south, and oars help for either direction. We also saw men fishing from simple skiffs made of papyrus stalks bound together with ropes. I learned that papyrus stalks are filled with air pockets, which is how those things manage to float. Boats have never been part of Abi's and my life. I'd gotten used to eating fish regularly while in the harem but had not thought much about how they are caught. We sometimes eat fish in Canaan but being back with my own people again meant a change in diet. Like most women, I have my own way of cooking and seasoning food. At last, I could have a red meat stew, seasoned the way I like it!

Ta-Sherit's hair grew in, over time. In the typical Egyptian style for children, most of her head was shaved, except for a long, braided lock hanging to one side. The Egyptians call it the "Lock of Youth" and frankly, I think it looks silly. But I certainly did not have any say about how Senbi's child or any other Egyptian child should wear his or her hair. I told Ta-Sherit she would not need to wait until her first blood before growing all of her hair long, and that she could cut her Lock of Youth anytime she wanted to have it the same length as the rest of her hair. She was pleased to be offered this early promotion to adulthood. I was pleased to see her beautiful hair growing in, thick and shiny, and I have to admit I did enjoy braiding her long lock, despite the overall look of the hairstyle. She's such a beautiful girl.

I had a lot to catch up on. Our household included many more people and we owned much more livestock. I was the wife of the patriarch and I needed to become re-acquainted with our original household and to meet our new people. Along with the camels came a mischievous camel herder boy, Gobi. Lot had found a wife: an Egyptian woman named Adoth. She was a city girl who never fully adjusted to our life on the move. She had a hard time leaving Pharaoh's city; I think she always wanted to return to Thebes. She kept looking back, even after the city was no longer visible in the distance. I figured out that Adoth was the link between our camp and the Egyptian officials, and thus the source of the information that eventually reached Pharaoh that I was Abram's wife, not his sister. Thank you, Adoth; you have no idea how important a role you played in my life. I met the new servants, saw the new livestock, and became familiar with the new household equipment while supervising the constant packing and unpacking as we moved out of Egypt.

I also caught up on who was expecting a baby. I had a joyous sense of fulfillment as I reclaimed my old role of midwife and pregnancy advisor. Of course, I had delivered a few babies during my time in the harem, but at last I would be doing my work for the house of Abram rather than for the house of Pharaoh. I prayed that I'd soon be delivering my own baby. Having my own baby was the most important goal as I transitioned back into my old familiar life.

I spoke to Jokim, who had been part of our household for a long time and whose first child I had delivered before we went to Egypt. She'd had another two while in Egypt and was pregnant again. "I'm so glad to know I'll have you with me again this time, Sarai," she told me. "You did well by me. The Egyptian midwives are not like the midwives of our people. They are, shall we say, not vigorous; you might give birth before an Egyptian midwife even moseys along to help you."

"Oh! Those Egyptians! I can imagine you had a bad experience, dear Jokim. I promise I will do my very best for you. I thank El Shaddai that I am back with my own people, doing what I'm good at doing."

Abram's nephew Lot had become more mature during the time in Egypt. Sometimes I would see flashes of his grandfather Terah in him. But I always thought Lot was a thin shadow of his grandfather. Terah was a great man. I had always admired him, even back in Ur. My father had many friends, but Terah was the one I considered to be a second father to me. That was one reason my father gave me to Abram while Merai was given to Og. Of course, everyone expected that we daughters would follow the custom of moving into our respective husbands' households, which in this case meant me moving into the house of Terah. I was happy at the thought of being associated with Terah, and I had every expectation that Abram would mature into a fine man like his father. At that time, I didn't know Abram as well as I knew Terah, but no matter. Sometimes bride and groom meet on the wedding day. From what I'd seen of Abi before we married, he seemed to be gentle, sober, and serious. I, meanwhile, knew that I had the great asset of being beautiful—some said I was the most beautiful girl in Ur. So, I was fairly confident he would be pleased with me.

But Terah was supposed to go to Canaan; he only went as far as Haran. Just getting that far was quite an effort but I do not know why he did not follow through and complete the mission. Maybe his son Haran's death demoralized him. I had always thought it was just a coincidence that Terah's youngest son, who was born and died in Ur, was named Haran. But then we settled in a land that also happened to be called Haran. Maybe there was a connection. Maybe the name of our location was a constant reminder of his lost son. Terah's personality changed while we lived in Haran; he became passive. Perhaps he thought that a god who would let his son die should just do what needed to be done to get the family to Canaan without our having to make any effort.

Abram and I believe that people need to take action to make things happen once they know what the god wants. That ultimately is why Abi and I packed up our belongings and left Haran. Abram could have had a prosperous life there. He would have inherited a large amount of land from Terah. But El Shaddai wanted us in Canaan, so we had to take matters into our own hands to get there and to take care of ourselves in order to survive and accomplish whatever it was we were supposed to do there. El Shaddai did not send a chariot to pick us up and take us to Canaan in a whirlwind, which seemed to be what Terah was waiting for. That is the only negative thing I have to say about Terah: he was supposed to get himself and our whole family to Canaan, but he did not.

We journeyed on through Egypt, going back towards Canaan where El Shaddai had sent us in the first place. The trip to Egypt had been a disaster from my point of view, but Abi and I both survived it—and we really might not have survived the famine had we stayed in Canaan. And Abi had grown richer.

But all those years in the harem under the pretext of being his sister! I certainly wasn't happy about what Abi had put me through. I don't think Terah would have done that. I could only comfort myself with the belief that Abi learned he had done wrong and that he was embarrassed about my having been in Pharaoh's harem. Plus, when Pharaoh castigated Abi in front of a bunch of women, that must have hurt his pride. El Shaddai didn't like what Abi had done, either. But fortunately, El Shaddai acted on the displeasure by smacking Pharaoh with plagues, while making Abi rich. I can't say I understand our god's idea of justice, but I am glad Abi wound up on the right side of that one.

I could see my husband did not want to hear about what I'd been through during the last several years. So, I never told him about the badly ended pregnancy. I didn't tell him about Bee-bee and Hakkin, or that Ta-Sherit was their child. Better to let him think that Ta-Sherit was just some

Egyptian servant girl. It might not be a good idea to let Abi or anyone else know that men visited the harem, thus raising suspicions that Bee-bee wasn't the only one with a lover on the side. On the other hand, our household might be highly amused to hear how Pharaoh had been duped, but I didn't think it was worth the risk. I never told Ta-Sherit all the details of her background, either. At first, she was too little to understand it, and then as the years passed, there just wasn't much reason to bring it up.

Ta-Sherit knew that she was Egyptian, and she let everyone know it. She was always proud of being Egyptian—Egypt was an important, ancient, and advanced civilization and she liked to think of herself as Ta-Sherit the Egyptian. She was especially proud of Egypt when we had traveled far enough north to be able to see the Great Pyramids at Giza. They are on the west side of the Nile and we traveled on the east side, but they are big and impressive, hard to miss even across the river. Of course, the pyramids are not very far from the shore of the Nile, since once they brought those large stones by river, it would be difficult to move them very far inland. Abi and I had noticed the pyramids years before on our trip south, fleeing the famine in Canaan, but admiring architectural marvels was not on our agenda. The soldiers moving us out proudly told us that the Great Pyramids were tombs for royalty who had ruled Egypt hundreds of years ago. Again, there was that fixation on death and being prepared for the afterlife rather than focusing on this life. Lot asked what the names of those rulers were, but the soldiers didn't know. Maybe immortality isn't all it's cracked up to be.

When we moved from Haran to the land of Canaan, Abi and I had seen the fortified city of Hazor, the largest and most important city in Canaan. It's located at a chokepoint in the foothills north of the Sea of Galilee in the Huleh Valley. It is on the only road through that area, so there's no way to enter the land from the north without passing through Hazor. Great for fee-collection purposes, right? The gates of Hazor were very impressive. But they were nothing compared to the Great Pyramids at Giza.

As Ta-Sherit grew up, she asked me about what it was like in Egypt, and I told her, as best as I could. I'd only seen the inside of the harem, and the route in and out along the Nile. She had a few memories of her mother, and I told her stories about Bee-bee, usually starting with, "Me and your mom . . . "

When she grew old enough to understand about fathers and mothers and rulers and multiple wives, she put the pieces together and assumed Pharaoh was her father. I didn't see much point in trying to tell her differently.

It would help her hold her own among our household, whether or not they were Egyptian, if they thought she was the daughter of Pharaoh. I was the only one around who had known her real father. And unfortunately, she did need a little help at holding her own among our household.

Once we were underway on our trip out of Egypt, it became clear that Ta-Sherit had no idea of how to live our new life. We were camping and constantly on the move. She had spent all her life in the harem, with the women. She'd never been around livestock. She'd never even seen anyone draw water, from the Nile or from a well. She didn't know how much work it was to carry water. Her idea of carrying water was to take a cup to someone across the room—she had been very sweet about doing so in the harem when asked. She did not know how to operate a well. She did not know how to identify a spring in the wilderness. Frankly, she never did get very good at that. She had no idea of how to set up a tent, never having seen one before. As for the animals, she did not know the biting end from the kicking end. She did not know that you had better not stand close behind a donkey because it might kick you. She didn't know camels can bite. "If it has a mouth, it can bite," I advised her.

It wasn't her fault that she didn't know these things. But the servants, who had grown up with all these skills, didn't understand. They just thought she was stupid. Lot was the only one who tried to help her adjust to our way of life. Lot and his wife liked children but had not yet had any. "Little girls are so cute!" he exclaimed when he first met her.

For example, he taught her the difference between a sheep and a goat. She'd heard of them, and had eaten both kinds of meat, but had never seen either on the hoof. "Tail up goat! Tail down sheep!" she danced around and chanted this lesson for days.

To keep her safe amid so many unfamiliar situations, I kept her with me and constantly told her what to do and how to do it. To everyone else, it simply looked like I was ordering my slave girl around. She was quite young and would not have been expected to do much of anything if we were back in the harem, but our nomadic and agricultural lifestyle is far more demanding. If you are old enough to walk, you are old enough to work—that's the rule for our people.

No one other than me was interested in her. So much of one's identity is based on who one's father is, and this little girl was essentially fatherless, Pharaonic claims notwithstanding. The one thing that was completely clear about her origin was that Abi was not her father. Some of the household might have suspected that Ta-Sherit was my daughter by Pharaoh, since I treated her maternally. But saying, or even thinking, that she was my daughter would involve concluding that Abram's wife had been impregnated by another man, an insult to his honor. And no one in our household dared to insult Abram's honor.

One might think it would give her some level of status to be seen as Pharaoh's daughter, regardless of who the mother was. But Pharaoh wasn't around to demand that she be respected, and he was not well-thought of among our household, anyway. Many of them simply referred to him as "The Foreigner," not even wanting to acknowledge his name or title. They pronounced the words "The Foreigner" in a mocking way that they imagined to be an upper-class Theban accent, so it came out sarcastically as "ha gaaar" instead of our usual term for the foreigner, "ha ger." Even the workers we picked up in Egypt took to calling him that. Egyptians who wound up as our workers were not the ones who had benefitted from the affluence of the Egyptian ruling class. Ta-Sherit came with me from the harem, so the most natural assumption for our workers to make was that she had been my servant there.

Ta-Sherit, however, was a little girl and didn't understand any of that. She had only ever lived in the palace, where Pharaoh was honored as a god, and where it was obvious to everyone that Egypt was the pinnacle of civilization. Ta-Sherit constantly reminded everyone that she was Egyptian, and that she was the little daughter of Pharaoh. Adoth thought this was cute, but everyone else thought it was annoying. So, the workers referred to her as the little daughter of the foreigner, which eventually was shortened to "Hagar." I didn't call her that and I made sure that Abram, Lot, and Adoth knew her proper name. But I could only do so much about the workers using the nickname, especially when I wasn't around. She had a perfectly good name, a pretty name for a pretty girl, and I wished people would use it.

This trip from Egypt to Canaan was probably the first time in her life that Ta-Sherit had been truly thirsty. I hate to say anything negative about Abi, but he really was kind of stingy with the water. His body's thirst level was somehow different from that of other people. He simply didn't need as much water as other people do. So, he thought the small amount that he needed was adequate for others as well. And of course, we spent most of our lives moving around and not always knowing when or where we would find the next well, or whether there would be a quarrel about our using someone else's well. Water is heavy to carry around. It makes sense to be parsimonious with the water, but in my opinion, Abi overdid it.

Once the soldiers got us across the Sea of Reeds, we would be on our own to get back to Canaan. We planned to travel by the Way of the Sea, the usual route along the southeast coast of the Great Sea. But our Egyptian escorts had a hard time finding a way around and through the swampy land. "Pharaoh told us to go this way. Our orders are to get these people to the other side of the Sea of Reeds. Pharaoh seems to think I have some kind of magical power to just hold up my staff and dry up the swamp so we can walk through this muck!" the officer in charge said in exasperation to another soldier.

But we found a way out and made our exit from Egypt.

Chapter 9

ONCE WE WERE THROUGH the muck of coastal Egypt and rid of our Egyptian escort, we proceeded east, then north. Eventually, the landscape became more like what we were accustomed to in Canaan: dry. The first time we came to a well, I showed Ta-Sherit what it was all about.

"This is a well. Wells are very important. We get drinking water for ourselves and for our herds and flocks," I began. "A well will have a cover, often a stone, and sometimes there is a stone trough nearby that you can fill so it's easier for the animals to drink."

"That looks like a hard way to get water. Why don't you just get water from the Nile?"

"We are moving away from the Nile. There isn't going to be any Nile in the places we live."

"But the Nile is the source of life," she said, repeating the standard Egyptian understanding of the world. "How can we have life if we are far from the Nile?"

"You need water to live," I explained, "but there are many rivers and sources of water other than the Nile." I thought of my home city of Ur on the Euphrates, but that seemed a bit complicated to explain to her just then. "Once we get through this desert area, the landscape changes and it's much greener. Sometimes we move the flocks and herds to an area watered by a river called the Jordan. Also, there are streams called wadis that have water in the rainy season but are empty in the dry season. The rainy season is during the cool winter months and the dry season comes in the hot summer months."

"What does 'rainy' mean?"

Oh, she's Egyptian, all right. And she has hardly ever gone outdoors. "Rain is water that falls down from the sky."

"Really? That can happen?"

"Yes, it can. Some parts of Egypt get rain, like along the coast of the Great Sea, but it doesn't really rain around Thebes where we used to live."

"Water falling out of the sky! I can't wait to see that!"

Wait 'til she sees snow, I thought.

"Is the Jordan River as big as the Nile?"

Ha! She was going to be disappointed when she saw it. "No. But there are no crocodiles in it either. Right now, let me show you how to use the well. The men have already taken the cover off. That is probably too hard a job for a little girl like you, but you will grow bigger and stronger. Then, take your container, which might be a clay jar or one made of animal skins like this one, and it's on a rope and you let it down into the well. It fills with water and you haul it up. Sometimes it takes a while." Indeed, the water level in this particular well was rather low. It was a lot of work to haul it up. I realized I had lost strength in my arms and back during my wasted years of lounging around in the harem. Getting back into my old way of life was going to be tough.

"Sometimes there is water in a well even if you think it's dry, even if other people tell you it's dry." Life is like that, I thought. Sometimes you can make a way even when it looks like there is no way. You might as well try, you should pray, you can hope, because sometimes people are wrong when they claim you can't do something. And sometimes you are wrong when you think you can't. But I also thought Ta-Sherit was too young to understand the metaphor, so I returned to practicalities. "You usually have to carry the water back to the tents or somewhere. You can carry it on your head, on your shoulder, on your hip, whatever works best for you with the container."

"Sounds hard. We used to have servants bringing us fresh water."

I hoped she would forget about our old life. Rather than argue the merits of one lifestyle versus the other, I told her about the etiquette and culture of well use: that many different people, including travelers, use the well, so wells can be places of social gathering and that wells can serve as landmarks: wells don't move around. I thought I should save for another day a discussion of how controversies can arise over well use, how some-times our household needs to move on from good grazing land because someone won't let us use what they consider to be their well.

"Sometimes when you are at your usual well, someone you can tell is a stranger may come, needing water. You should draw for him and for his animals," I explained.

"Why should I have to do that for someone I don't even know?" she pouted.

"Hospitality."

"Is that the name of a god?"

"No. But maybe it should be." Hospitality is important to our way of life. It wasn't an issue, or perhaps I should say, wasn't even a possibility, living in the harem of Pharaoh. I wanted Ta-Sherit to learn the practice of hospitality as the normal way to treat other people, before hearing about the grim consequences of its occasional absence.

"Why would a god care about what I do for other people? Gods care about what we do for them, not for other people."

"You do it because next time you might be the one who needs water."

"But the person who I helped wouldn't be the same person who could help me some other time and place."

"You help a stranger because you never know who that stranger might turn out to be. You might miss out on a great opportunity." I could see she didn't think much of this explanation, but her argument did make me wonder if El Shaddai was interested in how Abi and I treated other people. We had received instructions to move to Canaan, and a promise of land and descendants. And—maybe—instructions to say I was Abi's sister. But nothing about how to deal with other people. Would that come later? Or was it just about our relationship with El Shaddai?

Since I had noticed that the water level in the well was quite low, I had an idea to try to teach Ta-Sherit something about faith. I took a cup and filled it with water from the skin. I let her pour it back into the well, telling her to wait and listen. It was a long moment before we heard the water that she poured splash into the water below.

"You see, Ta-Sherit, during the time that the water is falling, you don't hear anything. But while you are waiting, you can know that you will hear it; you can be absolutely sure that it will get there. It always does. And that is what it is like with the god my husband and I worship: we have faith that what god told us will happen, will happen. Just like that water will hit bottom and splash. Faith is what happens in the time in between pouring and hearing." I paused and admitted, "Sometimes it is hard during the waiting, though."

I'm not sure how much of this she absorbed, but you have to start somewhere. She wanted to keep pouring more cupsful down, so I let her do it just one more time. I'd worked hard to draw that water up.

Complicated Family

Chapter 10

.

YEARS WENT BY. WE kept moving; I kept not getting pregnant. I was back to living life in fourteen-day segments. Blood. Aching disappointment. Waiting for the next fertile time. This time it will work. Get Abi to take that opportunity. Hope. Hope. Hope. Hope. Hope. Hope. Hope. Hope. Hope. Hope. Hope. Hope. Hope. Blood. The weeping of an achingly disappointed womb. Try again next time. Had I ruined my womb? Had it rotted because of what I did? I could never get away from the haunting feeling that the pregnancy I hadn't wanted might have been my only pregnancy.

The land and livestock also had their cycles. Planting, harvesting. Wheat, barley. Moving the flocks and herds. Sheepshearing. Breeding. Birthing. Each year a version of the previous one, some more prosperous than others, but overall, much the same.

I had a lot to do to raise Ta-Sherit, and I did it for the most part on my own. I remembered how Merai and I had expected that we would raise our children together, back in Ur. That didn't work out as planned. I wondered what it would be like if Bee-bee were here with us, raising her own daughter. Bee-bee was from a working family; she must have had to work with her family for years before they sold her. I wondered how much of their way of working and living was like ours. They must have had some animals, but primarily they raised crops. They likely drew their water from the Nile or an irrigation ditch filled by the Nile, rather than using a well or spring. Even if Bee-bee were here, I'd be instructing Ta-Sherit in how to live the way we do. But Bee-bee was no more here with us than Merai was.

So many transformations to teach my girl: How to turn sticks into a fire. How to turn cold water into hot water. How to turn a live animal into a dead animal. How to turn a dead animal into raw meat. How to turn raw meat into food. How to turn olives into oil. How to turn grapes into wine. How to turn milk into cheese.

How to turn grain into beer. They do it differently in Ur, where I first learned how, from how they do it in Egypt. Abi liked it the Ur way, so I made it that way for him. Other women in our camp made it the Egyptian way or some other way they had learned in their homelands. I taught Ta-Sherit the Hymn to Ninkasi, which my aunt had taught me, so long ago in Ur. I downplayed the part about Ninkasi being the goddess of beer and just explained her as being a woman from long ago who invented beer in Sumer. The song has a steady rhythm, which makes it easy to remember the recipe. It's not like I, or my aunt, or anyone we knew, could write it down and read it later. So, we remembered it as a song. The usefulness of the Hymn to Ninkasi is how I got the idea to organize my learning about pregnancy, childbirth, and lactation into a series of songs.

How to shear a sheep. Men usually did this, getting together for a drinking fest while they were at it, but a woman needs to know how to do it, too. How to card wool. How to spin carded wool into thread. How to set up and use a loom. How to weave thread into cloth. How to set up a tent. How to take down a tent. Where to set up a tent.

Herbs! Which ones are good for what. Which ones are good for nothing. How to turn them into teas, solutions, oils, pastes, ointments.

In the ordinary routine of getting through each day, turning one thing into another, the most amazing transformations of all occurred: I turned into a mother and a little girl grew up.

Sometimes, something out of the ordinary happened. The two most notable events from that time both had to do with Lot. Abram and Lot had each acquired and bred so many animals in Egypt that the arid hard-scrabble terrain of Canaan could not support them all. Abi and Lot were getting along perfectly well. But the herders who worked for each of them caused problems, competing for resources. Damascan Eliezer, our steward, decided on the work assignments. He had divided up the herders and designated some as responsible for Abi's herds and others as responsible for Lot's. So, when it became clear that the entire household was too large for the land to sustain, the lines between the two groups of herders, along with their respective animals, had already been drawn. The obvious solution was for Abi and Lot to separate.

Abi felt he had done his duty to his brother's son by getting him out of Haran and into the land El Shaddai showed him. "As long as Lot doesn't go back to Haran, I accept his choice," Abi said. And like the sweet guy that he is, Abi let Lot choose first where to go. Lot chose the plain of the Jordan River, in the direction of Zoar. It was really Lot's wife, Adoth, who was behind that decision. She was Egyptian, and she liked the look of a plain that was well-watered by a river, the way it is in Egypt. Also, she wanted to live in one of the cities of the plain, since she was a city girl at heart. So, they moved their tents to the outskirts of Sodom. Adoth did not care whether the folks there were interested in our god. She herself was still worshipping Egyptian gods when Lot wasn't looking.

After they left, Abi and I received another message from El Shaddai telling Abi, again, that all that land, visible in all directions from where we were, would be given to him and his descendants. Again, we inhaled the scent of bright light and were overcome by that thrill, that energy, that indescribable feeling when we heard from El Shaddai. I was greatly relieved that we heard anything at all from our god. This was the first message since that time in Shechem at the oaks of Moreh, before the famine, before we went to Egypt. Abi and I had worried that we had lost favor by doing something wrong. Or lost favor for no reason at all. After all, we had gained favor in the first place for no reason whatsoever.

Since we wound up richer when leaving Egypt than we had been when we entered, it wasn't clear that the journey to Egypt was the mistake, or whether the problem was that the journey wasn't a quick in and out. I thought the mistake was in Abi's wife-sister scheme and sending me to Pharaoh. Our god had caused trouble for the Egyptians because of that, so my presence in the harem clearly was the source of the displeasure, as opposed to the mere fact of our traveling to Egypt. I did not hear from our god the whole time I was in the harem and neither did Abi. But El Shaddai was communicating with us again, so we were grateful to learn that leaving Canaan had not broken the relationship.

Abi and I, meanwhile, would have liked more information about our having descendants. Please? I was offering sacrifices and wondering and praying about how that was supposed to work, because it wasn't working in the normal way. I was relieved, however, that the sojourn in Egypt had not negated the part about descendants. The ill-fated pregnancy caused me a great deal of grief and worry about my having children with Abi in the future.

But there we were with a confirmation of what we had been told previously: land for us and our descendants. We moved on to Hebron and built a stone altar near some oak trees. I loved that area and was very happy living there. Abi and I became friends with three fun-loving Amorite brothers who lived there: Mamre, Eschol, and Aner. We had great times together with them and their wives, drinking wine and telling stories around the fire at the end of the day. "Eschol" is a nickname meaning "grape cluster." People called him that because he was skilled at making wine. He made some of the best wine I've ever had, in or out of Egypt.

Another unusual event that occurred around that time had to do with Lot. While Lot was living in Sodom, some of his belongings were stolen, mostly food and household goods. Lot went after the gang that robbed him, which turned out to be not such a great idea because they kidnapped him! When Abi heard about it, he asked Mamre, Eschol, and Aner to go with him to try and negotiate a deal to get Lot back. They took silver and weapons with them, not sure which would be the better tools for negotiation.

They travelled for two days towards the northeast from where we were in Hebron and found the thieves camped in the wilderness on the west side of the Dead Sea, not even as far as Jericho. It was during the new moon, a very dark night; no one could see anything. But Lot recognized Abi's voice calling for him and found his way to him. Mamre, Eschol, and Aner split up from each other and they grabbed whatever stuff they stumbled upon.

The gang of thieves was just a miscellaneous bunch of Amorite riff-raff from the region to the east, bossed around by a minor warlord named Chedorlaomer. The rest of the gang resented him and didn't trust him. They were an every-man-for-himself kind of crew. In the darkness and the confusion of four people separately re-taking their captive and their stolen possessions, Chedorlaomer and his gang wound up attacking each other. Abi, Lot, Mamre, Eschol, and Aner all got away without a scratch!

One could say that the rescue expedition ended well: they recovered Lot and they collected some loot. But the story didn't end there, and it didn't end well enough for some people's taste. It's absolutely incredible how that episode was exaggerated in the retelling. After Lot was safely back home in Sodom, the other four of them told the story over and over, embellishing a little bit more each time.

The distance they travelled in pursuit of the gang of thieves was ripe for exaggeration. I have heard versions of this story where they pursued the thieves as far as Dan. Dan! Do you know how far Dan is from Hebron? And then that they chased them all the way to Damascus. Hilarious! Why not all the way back to Haran?

It was such a great story, it became legendary. People who heard it once wanted to hear it again and again. Listeners liked it so much that they knew every detail and imagined themselves being in on the adventure. Some started to believe they truly had been along on the escapade. (Consumption of wine helped with this disconnect from reality, by the way.) Some of them had not even been born when it happened! Abi and the three brothers always had such a good time telling their story. They didn't want to disappoint their listeners by saying that, no, it had just been the four of them; the listener had not been there. Last time I heard this story, there were three hundred and eighteen men in on the rescue. And that was three hundred and eighteen trained men! Yeah, right, we always travelled with an army. Hilarious!

Oh, and the Amorite riffraff turned into the kings of here, there, and anywhere, just to make their downfall even more impressive. Authentic-sounding personal names for the kings, formerly anonymous thieves, were made up, as were names for their non-existent kingdoms.

And on the topic of non-existent kingdoms, there also was Melchizedek. That man did not need embellishment. I've never met anyone else even remotely like him. He dressed up like a king, although he had no kingdom, and announced himself as a priest of El Elyon and went around blessing people. He was such a nice man: calm and composed, generous with the bread and wine, and radiant with goodwill. It just made you happy to be around him. That, by itself, is a blessing.

Melchizedek seemed to know something about our god, but Abi and I couldn't figure out how. It made me wonder if our god was communicating with other people, not in our family, and blessing them, too, or giving them the power to bless others. The name that Melchizedek used for god, El Elyon, means the Most High god, and it fit squarely with what Abi and I understood about the god we called El Shaddai. God Almighty, Most High god, I wouldn't be surprised if there were ninety-nine beautiful names of our god. And even so, could any number of words fully describe something indescribable?

Melchizedek spoke of god as the maker of heaven and earth. Abi and I had not thought of that, to tell you the truth. We were still trying to figure out this mysterious god of ours. We had caught on that he (if in fact this god was a he, not a she . . . or maybe both?) was not the god of, say, the sun, the moon, a river, etc. We sensed the power when El Shaddai spoke to us. But we hadn't thought of our god as having created everything. We were just trying to make our way through the day-to-day, season-to-season, and in my case, month-to-month, challenges of our lives. And sometimes we wondered about the larger issues of how god's promises to us of land and descendants would be fulfilled. We had never really thought about the origins of the heavens and the earth and who had made them. Abi and I were grateful to King and Priest Melchizedek for revealing that aspect of our god to us.

Ten years in the land of Canaan. It was a lot of fourteen-day segments, more than I want to try to count. Sometimes time is cyclical; sometimes time's arrow goes in only one direction. Abi grew older. I grew older. My pretty little girl became a beautiful young woman.

Chapter 11

ONE DAY TA-SHERIT FOUND me in my tent and asked me to come with her to get water from the well. I knew this wasn't about water; I knew she wanted to talk. The walk to and from the well usually took enough time to discuss whatever problem had arisen. So, I picked up a water jar even though I was feeling rather old to be lugging water around.

When we reached the well, we each took a drink and I sat down to rest while she drew water and filled her large jar and then my smaller jar. I knew my girl well enough to be able to tell when something was bothering her. But I had no preparation for what she asked me.

"What if I were Abram's second wife and had his child for you?"

I knew about this kind of arrangement. People do it. In fact, during our travels I had delivered a few babies conceived this way. Way back on our journey from Ur to Haran, we had gone through a territory—I think it was called Nuzi—where the custom dictated that a barren wife was expected to provide a substitute woman to ensure children for her husband. Each time I had delivered a baby who had two mothers due to an arrangement like this, the barren wife was very particular about everything being just right during the delivery and often wanted to assist me as midwife, whether or not she knew anything about delivering babies. But although everyone knew that this was the way things worked in some families, Ta-Sherit's question was a shock to me.

"I'd rather do it myself," was all I could think to say.

"I know you would, Mama Sa-Sa. I know you are trying." She politely did not say anything about my deteriorating physical condition even though it was at that very moment affecting us: I was the one who needed to rest before walking back, not she, and she would be the one carrying the big water jar while I carried the small one.

"I'm just not as strong as I used to be, Ta-Ta."

"You're still beautiful, Mama Sa-Sa."

"Thanks. Being beautiful is better than the opposite, but it does some-times cause complications." I had another drink to prepare for the walk back. I still couldn't think of anything to say in response to her question except, "I'd rather do it myself." So I said, "Let's start back."

All these years, I'd been barren, and Abi never raised the possibility of taking a second wife. I was so grateful for that. During those long, dull, anxious years in Pharaoh's harem, I wondered if he might be with another woman. Of course, I was at Pharaoh's beck and call, so it wasn't as if I was chaste. But the big difference between my situation and his, if he was being unfaithful, was that it had been Abi's idea to send me into the harem. But here I was thinking about Abi and me, about our relationship, which was not an answer to Ta-Sherit's question.

She asked again. "Would you do this? I would take your husband and you would take my baby. But you would still have your husband."

"I would still have my husband. Abi and I have a lot of history together."

"The two of you breathe together. You are one spirit."

"We share the same root." I must admit I still like that aspect of Abi's dream, even if the dream was the source of so much trouble.

"Why do you want to do this?" I asked after a long stretch of walking in silence.

"I am old enough to be married. I am a daughter of Pharaoh of Egypt, and I should marry someone important." Ta-Sherit tossed her head and held it high.

Him again. Can we ever get away from Pharaoh and Egypt? Ta-Sherit was right about being of marriageable age. She was a beautiful young woman, with a lovely, slender figure and a graceful way of moving. The household of Abram was a few hundred people. Do you think none of them noticed? There was one worker in particular, Gobi, one of the camel han-dlers, who noticed. Not smart, not good at his work, not an upstanding character and pretty much a brute; I could see he would never make a good husband. But he was Egyptian, and Ta-Sherit was Egyptian, and he seemed to think that gave him a special claim on her. So far as I knew, he was the first man to pay attention to her, and I figured that being young and new to all this, Ta-Sherit was flattered and amused. I don't think she actually had any interest in Gobi, but she was willing to let him pay attention to her. I didn't want that loser marrying my girl. I wanted to get her into a better situation. But I had not given serious thought as to who that might be, and I certainly had not thought it would be my own husband.

But what did this have to do with her wanting to be Abi's second wife? "Being a second wife is not the greatest thing, you know."

"I know that is often the case. But my other mother was, what, nineteenth wife of Pharaoh? And she didn't have so bad a life. It's more a matter of who the husband is and who the first wife is. And I get along with you."

Walking helped me think. "You have other options, Ta-Ta. Would you want to marry Damascan Eliezer? He is an important man." Damascan Eliezer was still Abi's steward, manager of all our servants, and resolver of disputes among them. He determined the work assignments and typically, his word was the final word. Abi didn't like to disappoint anyone, so he avoided getting involved in resolving disputes. Damascan Eliezer was second in authority only to Abram in our household. He was good at his job and there was no one who was fit to replace him.

"Yuck. No." Then she gave a short unpleasant laugh. "But you are right, Mama Sa-Sa, there are few who are not under his authority."

"Anyone else in our camp?"

"No."

I was glad she did not mention Gobi. "But our camp is not the whole world. Anyone among the Canaanites around here? Would you like me to look?"

"No."

There might be men among Abi's relatives in Haran who were looking for a wife, I thought. I couldn't even remember how many sons Abi's brother Nahor had, or whether they were marriageable. But then Ta-Sherit would have to relocate to Haran. I did not want to lose her. And according to our god's initial communication to Abi, getting out of Haran had been the whole point.

"What about Lot? Would you want to be Lot's second wife? He is not too far away. Maybe he would even come back and join us."

Lot and Adoth were living in Sodom at that time. One might wonder how Lot, who spent his whole life as a nomadic herdsman, wound up living in a city. Adoth never took to our way of life and after much weeping she finally convinced Lot to settle in a city. Therefore, Lot was a relative who was reasonably nearby. He had two daughters but no son, so no help there.

"No. And Lot is gone; he is not coming back." She was right, of course. "You spend too much time in the future hoping for things that aren't going to happen."

Ouch. "Are you sure this is what you want, Ta?" Stupid question on my part. She was very definite about what she wanted and had just summarily rejected all the alternatives I had offered.

"I know what I want." And then, "If I am given to Abram and I have his child for you, it solves both our problems."

She was right. It would solve my problem of not having a child, although "I'd rather do it myself" was still all I could think. I want to solve my problem; I don't want her to solve it. But "both" our problems? Was there more going on with her? The mere fact of her being of marriageable age was not by itself a problem. Was Gobi causing a problem for her? If he was taking liberties with her—if he took the most important liberty with her—the standard recourse was that he would be compelled to marry her. And he would be quite satisfied with that; he would have a beautiful young wife.

Ta-Sherit had no father (sorry, Pharaoh, this time you just don't count) who could refuse Gobi and demand that Gobi pay him the bride-price instead. Because she was fatherless, he might not even have to pay anyone the bride-price! Ta-Sherit would be stuck with that worthless oaf. She said the reason for wanting Abi was because he was important. Nothing could protect her from being hassled by another man like being married to Abi would. Certainly, I wanted to save Ta-Sherit from an unfortunate fate as Mrs. Gobi. But was this the only way to do that?

"Is Gobi making unwanted advances?"

"It's not what you think." And then, "I don't want to talk about it."

I could understand her not wanting to talk about that. If anything happens, it's the woman's fault. A man hassles her, and people say it's her fault because she tempted him. I can't think of a time when there was a he-said-she-said controversy about whether the woman consented, when the woman was believed. It's one of the things that is always the woman's fault. Although I had a good opinion of Damascan Eliezer's sense of justice, he, like anyone else, would blame the woman. Maybe I'd better keep Ta-Sherit close to me, so Gobi won't be able to get to her alone.

"Abi is such a sweet old guy. He always wants to see the best in everyone. But if it's my word against Damascan Eliezer's, Abi's going to see the best in him, not in me," she murmured.

My mind kept returning to the thought that I'd rather have Abi's baby myself. The rest of the walk home was not long enough to think of alternative solutions. That night as Ta-Sherit and I slept in my tent, we lay on our sides, curled up spoon-style, with me on the outside and my arms wrapped around her, even though she was taller than me. I thought of her mother; I thought of my sister. But I didn't think of any way to solve her problem. Or mine.

I was still trying to figure out what El Shaddai meant when he told Abi he would have many descendants, exceedingly numerous. How were we to get to that future from where we were?

Eventually, I concluded that if it were supposed to happen in the obvious, normal way—that is, Abi making me pregnant and me giving birth—that would have happened already. That is what we had been working on for a long time. You stick to your plan until it doesn't work and then you try something different. So, I concluded that it was supposed to happen in some other way. Terah was supposed to have gone to Canaan but he didn't. Abram took action and went instead. If one thing doesn't work, something else does.

I remembered what I'd thought about in Egypt, about Pharaoh being the natural father of my baby while Abi would be the nominal father. I had rejected that possibility—and rejected the baby in a big and bloody way. Maybe I wasn't supposed to have done that. Had I ruined my womb? Had the Egyptian baby made my womb rotten? Maybe I was supposed to have had that baby. Maybe I had somehow invalidated the promise of descendants for me but not for Abi. How old would that baby be now, I wondered. Just about the same age as Ta-Sherit, of course, and old enough to be a father himself. I often felt like Ta-Sherit was a substitute for that baby. This time, was she supposed to be a substitute for me? And maybe this time something else was supposed to be the other way around: Abi the natural father, and me the nominal mother. And who better to be the birth mother than the woman who thought she was the daughter of Pharaoh of Egypt, who was also thought to be a god? It also occurred to me that maybe all the babies I had delivered, traveling from Ur to Haran to Canaan to Egypt and back to Canaan, were mine, somehow, and that is what El Shaddai meant about having a multitude of descendants. All these thoughts were swirling around in my heart. It was hard to figure out. "El Shaddai," I prayed, "silence all the voices in me except your own."

It took a long time for me to fall asleep.

Next day, back to the well. "Are you sure this is what you want, Ta-Ta? You really want to have Abi's baby for me?"

"Yes. I know what I want, Mama Sa-Sa. Are you willing to give me to Abram?"

"Yes. You may do this. I will talk to Abi." That's what I said, but all I could think was, "I'd rather do it myself."

I went to Abi's tent and said to him, "You see that El Shaddai has prevented me from bearing children. I don't know why, when he has promised us many descendants. El Shaddai must want this to happen in some other way. You should take my girl Ta-Sherit as your second wife. Maybe it is El Shaddai's plan that I will obtain children by her."

Abi listened to me as I told him my thoughts and about my conversations with Ta-Sherit, and he agreed to the plan. He said that he, too, wondered how the promise of many descendants would be fulfilled. "El Shaddai must want something to come about other than the ordinary way. Our god is not an ordinary god."

"One needs to know what time it is, including knowing when it is time to try something else."

Abi sighed. "I had always thought it would be you, Sarai."

"I had always thought it would be me, too."

Chapter 12

REPORTING BACK TO TA-SHERIT, I started planning. "Ta-Ta, where are you in your cycle?"

"Huh?"

"Your wedding night should coincide with your most fertile time."

"I don't feel more fertile any time more than another."

"Come on, Ta-Ta. We talked about this when I told you about your crossing the border to womanhood. You are most fertile fourteen days after the day your blood starts." Honestly, that girl . . . You would never guess she'd been raised by an expert midwife. "You need to know these things. You do remember when your blood started most recently, don't you?"

"Yeah. New moon. It was really dark that night and I had trouble seeing. Always the new moon. I am very much synchronized with Khonsu."

"Khonsu has nothing to do with it. Forget about Khonsu. But if you start at the time of the new moon, you will be most fertile around the time of the full moon."

"Oh."

So, I had a date and a wedding feast to plan. A big feast—kill quite a few of the fatted calves, mix the wine, arrange for musicians, all the other details involved in a celebration. We even cut some myrtle branches for decorations. We were a wealthy family, and we were going to do this up big. What about the neighbors? Yes, we will invite the local Canaanites, too. We sent a messenger to invite Mamre, Eschol, Aner and their families. Days of preparations and we were good to go. Ta-Sherit was beautiful, washed, and perfumed, dressed in her best clothes, and beaming from ear to ear, each of which was bearing a shiny gold earring Abi had given her as a wedding gift.

I brought out my beautiful inlaid wood cosmetics box, which I still had from my time in the harem. I had some kohl from Egypt, and I put it on her eyes, the traditional extended eyeline style. It made her eyelashes look even more spectacular. I also had some ground ochre to put on her cheeks. It had a little mica in it, so it was sparkly. She looked so glamorous. "You know, the last time I did someone's eyes with kohl, it was your mom's. Me and your mom used to do each other's makeup, hanging out in the harem." She looked like her mother, beautiful Bee-bee, at her best. "Your mother would be so proud to see you today."

"I love it when you tell me 'me-and-your-mom' stories."

"I have something special to give you today, Ta-Ta. This gold necklace was given to me by Pharaoh." (The tradition only speaks of gifts Pharaoh gave to Abi. Did you really think he never gave me anything?) The necklace was made of high-quality gold and was easily recognizable as being of Egyptian design. It was the finest piece of jewelry I owned, but I always felt ambivalent about wearing it.

"Thank you, Mama Sa-Sa. So that means Pharaoh touched it? I will treasure it always. I have never felt so much like a goddess as I do today."

"You look like a goddess," I said, although I wished she would let go of her Egyptian framework of gods and goddesses and understand what I'd told her, many times, about El Shaddai who spoke to Abi and me. But it was not the right time to get into that.

Abi was his usual pleasant self. It was a beautiful day, with the sun glinting off Ta-Sherit's gold jewelry. And it turned into a beautiful evening, as the sun set and the full moon rose. At that time, we were living in an area with a clear view both to the east and to the west, the round sun hovering at one side of the horizon and the round moon hovering at the other side of the horizon. And there we were, Abi and Ta-Sherit and I, in the middle of the world between the sun and the moon. Please, god, bless the three of us and the baby we long for.

During the feast, I got up to make sure the servants were bringing out more wine and meat, and I overheard one maidservant say to another, "It's a great day, isn't it?" and the other replied, "Yes, for everyone except the Damascan, who now will have to keep his grabby hands off The Foreigner. I just hope he doesn't go after my daughter now instead." And then, I got it. It wasn't about Gobi, it was about Damascan Eliezer. And then, I saw the bigger picture. It wasn't just about Ta-Sherit securing Abi's protection from unwanted physical attention. If Ta-Sherit produced an heir for Abi, Damascan Eliezer would lose out on inheriting from Abi.

Oh, Ta-Ta, you are one smart girl! The powerless, fatherless girl who owns nothing can cause a powerful man to lose a huge fortune. Brilliant. Beaming from ear to ear. Too, too bad, Mr. Grabby Hands.

I went back out to the feast. "Have some more wine, Eliezer," I said, refilling his cup.

Chapter 13

WHEN I FIGURED OUT that Ta-Sherit was pregnant—and of course I was keeping track of days—I was thrilled. I knew before she did. I've never been so happy to see someone throw up her breakfast. Abi was overjoyed when Ta-Sherit and I told him. The three of us went out to select an animal to sacrifice as a thank offering. Ta-Ta wanted to be part of this and I wanted her there, but I did warn her that the smell of the burning meat, and any other smells, might seem unnaturally strong to her. And, of course, I was thrilled to use, at long last, my vast knowledge of pregnancy care for the good of Abi's baby instead of someone else's, as I had done for so many years. It was the culmination of my lifetime of learning. I wanted to make this pregnancy perfect.

And—can you believe it—when I told Ta-Sherit it was important to drink plenty of water during pregnancy, she said, "Yeah, like you know so much about it." She was wrapping her pale yellow scarf around her neck while she said this. I was furious.

I was outraged at her disrespect for my knowledge. I argued with her about the importance of drinking lots of water during pregnancy and while nursing a baby. The argument grew so heated that Abi overheard and intervened. He put in his opinion that he didn't see why Ta-Sherit should drink extra water. Of course! He never thought anyone should drink extra water! "A baby is made of flesh, not water," he opined. Ridiculous! Ta-Sherit gave me a so-there look through those long eyelashes of hers and flounced off.

Then I was furious with them both for not respecting the knowledge I had spent a long lifetime acquiring and which at last could be put to use for the good of Abi's baby. I felt wronged by Ta-Sherit for thinking I didn't know anything about pregnancy and blamed Abi for not telling Ta-Sherit to listen to me because I was an expert on this topic.

"The wrong done to me is because of you!" I snapped at him. "I gave my girl to you to have your child and when she saw that she had conceived, she belittled me and what I know. May god judge between you and me, which one of us knows more about pregnancy and childbirth!" I was so angry at him that I almost told him about my pregnancy in Egypt. (Glad I didn't, though, when I calmed down.)

I'll give Abi credit for recognizing his mistake. "You are right. You have been listening to women's lore about pregnancy for decades; you are an experienced midwife and you've been delivering babies all the way from Ur to Haran to here. You are the one in charge of your girl. Tell her what she should do. This baby is important to me and to our god, too. Do to her what you know will make the baby healthy and strong. Do as you see fit. You are the expert."

A few months later, Ta-Sherit and I had another run-in on the same topic. She wanted to walk up the hill with some of the other young women, chew some herbs and watch the moon rise. I forbade her. She needed to rest. She had been on her feet all day—it was the barley harvest time, and everyone, including her and me, had worked full out all day. I knew the next day was going to be a hard workday, too. So, I wanted her lying down, with her feet up, not going for a walk. You may also recall that I had experience with the effects of mystery herbs on pregnancy and I certainly didn't want her messing around with who knows what while pregnant. So, yes, I was "harsh" with her, as she would say. She was furious that I wouldn't let her go.

She didn't go out that night, but a few days later, to demonstrate that she could go where she wanted when she wanted, she ran away.

She ran away with Abi's baby inside her.

Somewhere, decades before, when we were on the move through somebody's tribal lands, a midwife I was working with told the mother, who had just had her first baby, that to be a mother is to commit to having your heart walking around outside your body for the rest of your life. I certainly understood that statement even more deeply years later when I had Isaac, but right then, not only was my heart outside my body, it was inside someone else's body, and had been kidnapped. Abi and I were frantic. The baby was gone. We prayed and sacrificed to god like we'd never prayed and sacrificed before.

Several days later, our prayers were answered.

Ta-Sherit came back to my tent, running as best she could, given her condition (surely she could not have run the whole way back, could she?)

shouting, "Mama Sa-Sa! I saw your god! The angel of god spoke to me! I saw god and am alive to tell about it! God told me about the baby! I saw! The god you call El Shaddai saw me! I call the god El Roi! He calls the baby Ishmael! God hears! God sees!" To say that her eyes were shining and her skin was glowing would be an understatement. I saw in her the ecstasy I had felt and had seen in Abi when we received messages. In her case, the ecstasy had already lasted for days during her journey home. My girl must have had quite an encounter with the holy.

We had such a feast when she came back! Once we sat her down and she had a chance to catch her breath, we got some food and water into her. She told Abi and me and everyone who had gathered around her what had happened, filling in the details of the joyous yet incomprehensible report she had already given. I had thought I would never again be so happy to see someone as when Abi came to get me out of the harem, but this was even better. Our promise from El Shaddai had walked off and then run back.

The whole household was curious to know what the angel said to her. "It happened in the wilderness, somewhere between Kadesh and Bered," she recounted. "I was thirsty and luckily, I found a spring, the one on the way to Shur. I was resting there and a man came to the spring, and asked me where I had come from and where I was going. I said I was running away from home and from you. The moment I said it I regretted it, because what if he was a slave trader or something and he would know how vulnerable I was? I also realized that I didn't really know where I was going, that 'Egypt' was not a specific destination and that I didn't know what I would do when I got there. Then he said, 'Ta-Ta.' That startled me because you are the only one who calls me that, and how would this stranger know? I looked at his face for the first time and was terrified. His eyes were flames of fire. His face was like the sun shining at its full brightness. The next breath I took, I sensed the light coming from him in a different way, I inhaled it and finally knew what you meant by 'the scent of bright light' and I knew it was not a man but an angel of god, your god that you had told me about. He was looking at me with those fiery flame eyes in his face like the sun, and I realized to my surprise that I was not harmed by looking at him. He said, 'You are Ta-Sherit, Sarai's girl. Go back to her. Do what she says because she knows how to take care of you and your baby.' I could feel the presence of god and I could feel my heart submitting to god. I would come back. And then he said that I would have so many descendants that they would not be able to be counted!"

The assembled group erupted in praise and excitement.

"Just like god told Master Abram!"

"How wonderful! What a blessing!"

"Good for you to be blessed with such a large family!"

When they quieted down, she continued. "The angel knew I had conceived and said I would bear a son. The angel instructed me to call my son Ishmael because god had heard my cry for help. Then the angel told me a prophecy about him: 'He will be a wild donkey of a man, with his hand against everyone and everyone's hand against him, living in conflict with all his relatives.'"

"Congratulations, Master Abram!"

"Ishmael! May god hear us all!"

"A son! What a great blessing!"

"Sounds like he'll be a fighter. Go get 'em Ishmael!"

"Nobody pushes Ishmael around!"

"God hears!"

Ta-Sherit continued her story. "The angel said my name, and suddenly I wanted to name god in response. 'El-roi.' It just popped into my heart and came out of my mouth. God of seeing. God who sees. God who sees me. Those amazing eyes. I could hardly believe that I had seen god and stayed alive after doing so."

We thanked god and praised god like we'd never done before for sending that angel to send Ta-Sherit back. I felt vindicated that the angel found my girl at a spring, the one that we then started calling Beer-lahai-roi, which means "well of the living one who sees me." She was getting water from a spring! Ta-Ta listened to me even when she wasn't listening. I wasn't surprised she was on the way towards Shur, which is near the border of Egypt, proud as she was of being Egyptian. I think her image of Egypt was of a place where you spend most of your time lounging around on cushions with your feet up, so maybe she was taking my advice on that point as well, despite outwardly rebelling against it.

Ta-Sherit's return from the spring in the wilderness marked the start of a very happy, harmonious period in our lives. Ta-Sherit herself had experienced who this god of ours was. I had told her many times about El Shaddai and what our god had told Abi and me, but she just shrugged it off. I guess I can't really blame her. It's like trying to tell someone about a vivid dream; you can never find the words to convey the experience. She'd had an intense enough experience of the presence of god that she felt that she could give another name to god: El Roi. Naming god! I felt so proud of my girl. I can't say she fully understood who our god is—none of us do—but her experience gave her a sense of the greatness, the glory, the power. She had a glow about her that lasted for days.

She had felt El Shaddai's power and therefore was amazed that she survived the encounter. Of course, she had to survive! She had Abram's baby inside her! And having been instructed by the angel to do so, she let me take care of her. After nearly losing her, I was ever more grateful to have the opportunity to do so. She seemed wiser and more settled after her encounter, as if she had closed the door on her rebellious period and now was focused on moving forward to motherhood. Her first night back, we slept curled up together like we had so many times before, and I could wrap my arms around not only her but also our baby. Ishmael! That was the best night's sleep I have ever had, after so many nights of worry. Praise god from whom all blessings flow.

Another benefit of the annunciation to Ta-Sherit was that we knew what to name the baby. Not surprisingly, once it became clear that Abram was going to have his long-awaited child, there was no end to suggestions as to what the child's name should be. Even Lot came over from Sodom and visited us to express his opinion. (Haran. No.) Having a definitive statement from El Shaddai saved us from having to listen to an onslaught of recommendations and arguments.

And yet, we kept ignoring another part of the prophecy. "Wild donkey of a man. His hand against everyone. Everyone's hand against him. Will live in conflict with all his relatives." No one wanted to hear that; easier to simply dismiss it as so much incomprehensible jawboning from an over-wrought angel. It was not what any of us wanted for our baby.

The prophecy made Abi nervous. He was concerned that maybe the angel actually had said something worse about what the child would do, and that Ta-Sherit was holding it back, out of fear that the child would be rejected. "I wonder if the prophecy said that the child would kill me?" Abi whispered privately to me. I don't know where he got an idea like that. "Sarai, would you please press her for more information?"

"I am confident that Ta-Sherit can accurately report what was said in the most important conversation in her life," I responded indignantly. I was proud of my girl. She was worthy of the honor of having an annunciation from god and worthy of the honor of being able to name god.

Chapter 14

THE BIG DAY CAME. Ta-Sherit showed great strength. We had talked so many times about what it would be like. When her contractions started, she came to me and our eyes locked. Neither of us said a word. We wrapped our arms around each other.

"Mama Sa-Sa."

"Ta-Ta."

"Sa."

"Ta."

"I'm scared," she whispered.

"Of course you are. You know it's going to hurt. But you do know something that no other woman knows when she gives birth. You know the baby is going to survive." She looked at me, curious, after wincing through a contraction. "You know this because god has already told you what your baby will be like as a man. You know he will survive to adulthood. Who else ever knew that when giving birth?" We both ignored the obvious: knowing the baby would survive to adulthood did not necessarily mean the mother would survive the birth.

Ta-Sherit smiled and put her head on my shoulder. We walked to my tent. I told the servants I had chosen to help me to get us what we needed: birthing bricks (much plainer than the heavily decorated ones I'd used to deliver her, I thought with a wistful smile), oil for me to use to massage Ta-Sherit, string to tie off the umbilical cord and a knife to cut it, a few reeds to suction the baby's nose and mouth, water for Ta-Sherit to drink, water to wash the baby and salt to rub it with, soft cloth to wrap him in, ointment to help Ta-Sherit's healing, soft lamb's wool for packing and bandages, and lots of clean straw.

As for the knife, it was Abi's favorite, an old flint one. He and I both had better knives, made of bronze. I would have preferred to use a bronze one, but Abi had asked me to sharpen his old flint knife and to use it for cutting the cord. Abi had had this knife for a long time and he wanted it used in connection with this long-awaited step into the new phase of his life. There were a lot of people who could sharpen a knife for him, but I think he asked me to do it because I was the only one who understood his sentimental desire to use that old thing.

Those items are more or less the usual equipment any midwife would gather to prepare for a birth. But I also asked one of the women to build a fire just outside the tent and start heating some water. In my decades of collecting and developing information about best practices for childbirth, I learned to do something that hardly anyone else did: just before the baby comes out, I wash my hands in hot water, as hot as I can stand it. I don't know why this helps and it doesn't have much effect on the ease of the delivery itself, but it increases the likelihood of good health afterward for both baby and mother. My best guess is that since the baby is used to being warm in the womb, it is more comfortable being received into warm hands. Of course, I wanted Abi's baby to have every advantage.

Ta-Sherit and I and a few of the servants who had some midwifing experience settled in. Delivering babies is my forte. I had delivered Ta-Sherit herself, and she knew that. I took deep breaths with her. I held her hands and stroked her hair and wiped the sweat off her face and gave her water. "My girl, my girl," I kept saying to myself. "My boy, my boy," she said, when she could talk between contractions. Hours of contractions, at first spaced apart, then closer together and stronger and stronger until they were like the waves we had seen crashing on the shore of the Great Sea and then felt hitting our bodies when we waded in. Waves crashing over your head, and you don't know if you can get clear of the wave you're in before the next one hits you. And you know there is nothing, absolutely nothing, that can stop the next wave from hitting you. Ishmael's head crowned. Ta-Sherit screamed.

"This is going just the way it's supposed to. Your body knows what it's doing," I assured her, even though I knew that assurance does nothing for pain.

Head, shoulders, knees, bottom, Ishmael. I had the honor of catching him in my warm washed hands. He wailed. She gasped. I exhaled. I tied the umbilical cord with string and cut the cord with Abi's old flint knife, as requested.

I wiped baby Ishmael and kissed him and admired his perfect little fingers, toes, legs, arms, ears. I handed the precious baby to the servants to wash him, rub him with salt and wrap him in soft cloth, all of them admiring him and kissing him while I turned my attention back to Ta-Sherit. She was exhausted. I was exhilarated. Ishmael was hollering. Perfect.

When we had attended to Ta-Sherit's immediate needs and had the bleeding under control, I turned back to Ishmael and his cluster of admirers. I calmed him and when he stopped squalling and his mouth relaxed, I saw that it was a beautiful mouth, with perfect bow-shaped lips, just like his father's. I gave him to Ta-Sherit and helped her get her nipple into his darling little mouth. I remembered the feeling I'd had nursing her, and only then did I start to cry. "I am going to try," I told myself. "I am going to try to nurse him." I prayed that I would be able to. A day later, when Ta-Sherit was sleeping, I got a chance. It didn't work. That is what one would rationally expect, but rationality isn't everything. I am glad I tried.

Abi had a son. At last! That was the most important thing, the goal I had been working towards all my adult life. It had been a long and circuitous route. I wish I could have done it myself. We got it done in a different way and here was Abi's boy! But despite our agreed-upon plan that this was my child, despite the legal and social traditions accepting this kind of surrogacy, and despite the love I already felt for this darling baby boy, I realized I would have to step back from raising him.

I knew in my heart that Ta-Sherit had run away because of me, and I still felt chastened by the experience. I'd been too overbearing. Then, I really did know more than she did, as I am an expert on pregnancy care, childbirth, and care of a newborn. But I will admit I don't particularly know more than anyone else about raising a child. I will take care of Ta-Sherit during her recovery; I will help her take care of Ishmael in the first few weeks; I will be available if she asks for help or advice. I will hold myself back from interfering in her raising Ishmael. Abi has a son. That is the most important thing. I must not screw this up.

Chapter 15

ABI HAD HIS LONG-AWAITED son and for years, our lives went well. Abi and I grew deeper in our gratitude to El Shaddai. One new moon night, with the sky so clear and the Milky Way so bright that we could see our shadows cast by its light, Abi and I were deep in meditative prayer. We experienced another message. The first thing I noticed was the strange sensation as I inhaled: the scent of bright light. I still can't explain what I experience when it happens any better than that. I had smelled it twice before: when our god spoke to us near the oaks of Moreh, and again after Lot had gone his own way and god told us to look around, he would give the land to us and our descendants, who would be as uncountable as dust. Abram had also experienced the same sensation in Haran when god told him to go to the land he would show him. Ta-Sherit had experienced it during her encounter at Beer-lahai-roi. With the second inhale, I also noticed the taste in my mouth. It was like the sensation of cool water in your mouth when you are thirsty, except it was sweet like honey. I opened my eyes and looked at Abi whose eyes were wide open, looking at me, awestruck.

"You feel it, too?"

"Yes."

Neither of us ever got used to the intense feelings that overcame us when El Shaddai gave us a message. But at this point in our lives, we knew a little bit about what to expect when we felt the glory of god. The glory felt like a presence, a weightiness, a heavy pressure on our bodies, not painful, but impossible to ignore. And then we heard. Since the sound of the words feels like it is both inside and outside of oneself, I later confirmed that Abi had heard the same words that I did.

"I am El Shaddai," the message began. We were told to live blamelessly. Our names would no longer be Abram and Sarai, but Abraham and

Sarah. There would be a covenant. Abraham would be the ancestor of a multitude of nations. Exceedingly fruitful. All the land of Canaan as a permanent possession. The sign of the covenant was circumcision. All the males among us. God would bless me. I would have a son. I would give rise to nations and kings.

At that point, what we were hearing was too incredible for Abi. He fell on his face and laughed out loud. Later, he told me that he was thinking to himself, "Can a child be born to a man of my age? Can Sarah bear a child at her age?" He was so dismissive of what he heard about me having a son that he asked for Ishmael to be blessed as his heir instead.

God said no. God said I would bear Abraham a son, to be named Isaac, in about a year. God would establish his covenant with this son. This covenant would be a permanent covenant with Isaac's descendants. God heard Abi's request and blessed Ishmael also, in a different way: he would be the father of twelve princes. He too would have a huge number of descendants. But the covenant would be with the son I would have, Isaac, and Isaac's descendants.

At the end of this communication, we had a sense of God going up from us. This mystical sense of the presence of God was so deep and satisfying that I did not want to come out of it. And maybe, in a way, I never did. I felt my sense of self dissolving—at least, temporarily—dissolving into what? Into unity with . . . something? The entirety of the heavens and the earth? It was a feeling of immediacy, that this wondrous and incomprehensible El Shaddai was right there, surrounding me and infused throughout me. The feeling, even more so than the other two times, was unlike anything I had ever known, demanding my attention, and filling me with awe. The intensity of the feeling was temporary, but once I had experienced it, I would never forget it or be the same.

It is not surprising that El Shaddai gave us new names. We were new people after the experience of this message. We had a new relationship with God, although we were not at all clear about what this covenant meant. God said circumcision was its sign, but that didn't explain what the covenant itself was.

After so many years of uncertainty and waiting, we felt like we were back on track to fulfill the mission God had given us long ago. I particularly noted that this was the first time one of God's promises came with a due date: "this season next year." As it turned out, we needed that absolute certainty of what El Shaddai had commanded, in order to circumcise all the men and boys. Oh no, that announcement was not well-received in our household. Some of the men ran away from our camp, and we never saw them again. Abraham said that if he could undergo it at an old age like ninety-nine, they could deal with it, too. I circumcised Abi—did you think I would trust it to someone else? Abi and Damascan Eliezer circumcised all the other men, Abi using his favorite old flint knife. Abi took care to circumcise thirteen-year-old Ishmael himself. I think he had not entirely let go of the idea that he would like Ishmael to inherit the covenant, whatever it might turn out to be, along with Isaac.

The annunciation of Isaac's birth was repeated to us. It should be no surprise that it happened near Mamre's oaks. Of all the places I have lived, that is my favorite. Abraham saw three men at a distance, and at first, he thought they were Mamre and his brothers. But no! A visit from three strangers, the strangest visit we ever had, even stranger than our visits with dear old Melchizedek.

Abi and I were still feeling the effects of our previous encounter with El Shaddai, and we were so grateful to have an opportunity to offer hospitality to anyone. I would like to think that we had always been as hospitable as anyone else, but we had taken to heart God's command to live blamelessly. We were not exactly sure what all that entailed—there must be at least six hundred rules one needs to follow to be blameless—but surely being hospitable to strangers is one of them. Abi told me what to bake, then he went out, selected a calf to be prepared, and served the rest of the meal, curds and milk. I stood near the tent entrance, listening in case Abi wanted me to do anything else for our guests.

Then one of our visitors said I would have a son. The next breath I took, I had the overwhelming sensation again and as my nostrils filled with that wonderful scent of bright light, a rush of thoughts filled my heart. This was El Shaddai. The other times it had been a voice. This time there was a man standing in front of me. It had been a man, or something in the shape of a man, for Ta-Sherit at Beer-lahai-roi, so we knew it could happen that way. Many people would consider his news to be laughable. Abi laughed out loud when he heard it during the previous message from El Shaddai. I was delighted to hear again that I would have the pleasure of becoming a mother, even though Abi and I were so old.

I laughed with delight, but not out loud; nonetheless the visitor knew what was in my heart as if he heard me when I laughed to myself, and heard the words I said to myself about Abi and me being old. That shocked me. I had been heard. I had been heard, even though I had not laughed or spoken out loud. There are so many times in my life when I have spoken and not been heard, but this mysterious visitor heard me when I did not speak. Did he know everything I thought? Did he know everything I had ever done?

The visitor asked, "Is anything impossible for God Almighty?" In fear and humility, I babbled something. His question has reverberated in my heart ever since.

Chapter 16

IN THE BRIEF PERIOD after the three mysterious visitors said I would bear a son but before I conceived, our God intervened to protect me through the actions of Ta-Sherit. It was a messy situation, shot through with misunderstandings, but also with good fortune. We had journeyed south from Hebron to the kingdom, if that's what you want to call it, of Gerar in the Negev Desert.

Some of the local people, both men and women, came to visit us. We women served the men their meal, then the women sat down together for our own dinner. After eating, we sat and drank and told stories, men in one group and women in another. Abi told the men about our years-ago trip to Egypt and how he had told Pharaoh that I was his sister, because he thought the Egyptians would kill him because of my great beauty. He told them that Pharaoh had taken me but then released me, giving him many gifts of livestock and servants. I think he was trying to impress our visitors with his wealth and with his advantageous connection to Pharaoh. Of course, he left out the details about how long I had been there, the plagues our God had sent in response and how angry Pharaoh had been about his lie. Abi complimented me on all the kindnesses I had done him in leaving Ur and then leaving Haran and journeying to so many places with him. Chatting with the women, I spoke of how we had come from Ur by way of Haran, that Abi's father Terah had been a friend of my father's back in Ur and that Terah was like a father to me. It had seemed like such a pleasant visit. We were glad to show hospitality to our new neighbors and were eager to form a good relationship with the residents of the area in which we were sojourning.

But somehow, there was a huge misunderstanding. I am not sure how the miscommunication occurred: was it due to the differences in our languages? Were our visitors too drunk to remember the story correctly? Had they told someone who told someone who told someone who told their king something that had only the slightest resemblance to what we'd actually said? A couple days later, King Abimelech of Gerar sent messengers to us, saying they had orders to take Abraham's beautiful sister Sarah back with them for their king. We were appalled, but they were armed.

"No! I'm supposed to conceive Abi's son Isaac! God said so! I can't be trapped in another man's harem again," I moaned to Ta-Sherit.

"We can't let this happen," Ta-Sherit hissed.

Abi said nothing.

"I have an idea. Play along with what I say," whispered Ta-Sherit.

Uh-oh. Where have I heard that before?

Ta-Sherit stepped forward. "I am Abraham's sister, Sarah," she said calmly. The men among our earlier visitors had not spent any time with her or me and therefore did not know who, exactly, they were looking for.

I can't know what they were thinking, but they may have had some idea that they were looking for a woman around Abraham's age and suspiciously announced, "We're taking the old lady, too."

Ta-Sherit laughed and said, "You mean my old nursemaid? Ha! Well, if you insist. Come along, dear."

"Yes, ma'am." I managed to choke out the words. It would have been funny if we hadn't been in so much danger. I snatched up the nearest thing I could grab, which happened to be a partly full wineskin. I didn't have any particular reason for picking it up; I just didn't know what else to do because I didn't know what we might want to have with us and they certainly weren't giving us time to pack.

The messengers put us on their donkeys and took us to the, well, I'll call it the residence of their king, a mud brick house. Was Ta-Sherit expecting something on the order of Pharaoh's palace? Was that why she'd been willing to step forward? What was she thinking? It was getting on towards dusk and I tried to pay attention to the terrain along the way so that I could identify landmarks to help us find our way back home if we could escape.

They left us alone in a room together. I was beside myself with fear, anger, dismay. "How can this be happening again?" I wailed.

"No one is getting raped tonight," responded Ta-Sherit grimly. And then, "Why did you bring that wineskin?"

"I don't know. I just grabbed the nearest thing I could reach."

"God may be helping us by giving you that idea. I had some of the wine from that skin the other night. It's very strong. It made my head feel funny and I had strange dreams. King Abimelech is going to get very drunk tonight and he's not going to touch either one of us."

No time to discuss a plan. King Abimelech came into the room and dined with us. Ta-Sherit took over, making sure he had plenty of our wine while she and I avoided it and drank a little of the wine the king's servants brought in. After dinner, he stood up quickly, lunged at Ta-Sherit and passed out.

Ta-Sherit smiled a nasty little smile and after a few moments, started whispering, using her best imitation of an upper-class Egyptian accent. "Abimelech. This is God. You are about to die. You are about to die because of the woman you have stolen. Because she is a married woman. You are about to die." She whispered this over and over.

Abimelech stirred and spoke in his sleep or stupor or whatever state he was in. "I am innocent, God. Do not destroy an innocent person. The man said she is his sister. She said he is her brother. I have integrity in my heart. My hands are innocent. Do not kill me, I beg of you."

Ta-Sherit smirked at me and continued her role-playing. "Yes, Abimelech, I know that you did this in the integrity of your heart. It was I, God, who kept you from sinning against me. I did not let you touch her. And you must not touch either one of them. Abraham and the woman are not brother and sister. They did not say that. Now, I command you: return both women to Abraham. Abraham is a prophet. If you return them to him, he will pray for you and you shall live. But if you do not return them to Abraham, know that you shall surely die." I could just barely make out that she winked at me in the dim light of the oil lamp. "You shall surely die. You and your wives and children and servants and all that are yours. Die. Die. Die."

I was still terrified. But I could acknowledge that this would be hilarious if my girl and I weren't the ones in danger. Where did Ta-Sherit get all this bravado?

The next morning, King Abimelech rose early, in terror and with a terrible headache. He called all his servants and told them of his frightening dream. Ta-Sherit and I stayed off to one side, silent and with our eyes modestly lowered. When his men heard about the conversation between their king and God, they, too, were terrified. I don't know why Abi thinks no one else but him fears God, just because other people don't communicate with God the way he does. Especially afraid were the men who had visited us and were suddenly realizing that they had misunderstood and conveyed incorrect information to their king. Ta-Sherit and I were not about to explain who said what and who got things mixed up; the less attention we called to ourselves, the better. I left the wineskin behind. It had some kind of fungus or mold or something growing on the opening.

King Abimelech assembled a generous gift and took us back home to Abraham, but he still felt the need to save face by justifying himself. "What have you done to us?" he demanded of Abi when we arrived. "What have I ever done to you that you brought such great guilt upon me and my kingdom? You should not have done the things that you did to me! What were you thinking?" I recalled hearing Pharaoh making more or less the same accusations to Abi so many years ago, back in the harem. I wasn't as thrilled to see Abi as I had been that other time, although I was relieved to be back home. But, having reestablished his integrity and good name, Abimelech handed Ta-Sherit and me back to Abi, presented him with sheep and oxen, and left some men and women to work for us during the time that we sojourned in Abimelech's kingdom. He officially gave us permission to settle wherever we liked on his land. He also thought to consider my reputation, or Ta-Sherit's reputation—I'm not sure if he ever figured out what relationship either of us had to Abraham—and announced in front of everyone that he was giving Abraham a thousand pieces of silver to completely vindicate any insult to a woman's honor.

Then Abraham prayed to God on Abimelech's behalf, which seemed to be a great relief to him and his accompanying men. Everything was amicably settled. Thereafter, our camp had good relations with his people. Eventually, Ta-Sherit and I even went out among the women of the kingdom and delivered their babies, as needed. We were particularly pleased to deliver healthy babies of some women who previously had only had stillbirths. But we did try to steer clear of the men.

As soon as Abimelech and his contingent left, I caught up with Ta-Sherit. "Thank you for rescuing me. You took a great risk for me."

"I'm just paying you back for when you rescued me. And I want God's will to happen. You need to have your son Isaac. And it must be clear to everyone that your son Isaac is Abi's child. God wants this, and you have told me that sometimes we need to take action to make God's will happen. So, I took action. You could not be kidnapped and held in some other man's house."

"Your plan was brilliant."

"I didn't know what would happen to me when I stepped forward. I recognized that I might be trapped for years, like you were in the house of Pharaoh. I didn't know you would come with me, or that you would have that wineskin. You know, I think there is something wrong with that wine. There are no grapes growing here in the desert, so all the wine we have with us now is left over from when we were in Hebron. It's been in the sun and sitting around for a while. Not only is that wine strong, it seems to be tainted in some way, inhabited by demons that possess your mind, or at least invade your dreams. God must have guided you to pick it up and bring it."

Once again, I marveled at the tension between divine intervention and human action. And the question "Is anything impossible for God Almighty?" ran through my heart.

Next, I went to my husband. I was not happy about this near-repeat of the wife-sister disaster. Did that man learn nothing from our experience in Egypt? "Abraham. About that bag of silver Abimelech gave you," I said in a no-nonsense tone of voice. "It's not yours. Don't spend any of it. Hold it for Ta-Sherit and leave it to her as an inheritance. Whichever one of us dies first, it then goes to Ta-Sherit." It wasn't a thousand pieces of silver like Abimelech had said; of course, everyone knew that was an exaggeration for the sake of appearances. My guess is that "one thousand" was the highest number he knew. But it was a good amount of high-quality silver, and I always had an eye on securing Ta-Sherit's future after Abi and I were gone.

Chapter 17

THIS MOST MIRACULOUS PHASE of my life happened in the most ordinary way. I became pregnant in a very ordinary way. My pregnancy was quite normal: morning sickness for a while, a good middle trimester, followed by growing bigger than I thought was humanly possible. My sense of smell intensified. I recalled that the same thing had happened when I was pregnant in the harem, but then it was usually perfume and incense, which were not the kind of smells that surrounded me in our camp. There are more bad smells than good smells in the world, I concluded. I took to chewing mint, when I could get it, to make my breath fragrant, so at least I could smell something pleasant.

Isaac quickened. The first time I felt him move, I nearly fainted with joy. It felt like the brush of the wing of a butterfly. Did Isaac feel my joy? Did the child in my womb jump for joy? I told Ta-Sherit and she hugged me. She said that all along, she believed the promise our mysterious visitors made to me would be fulfilled, and that she felt blessed for having believed it. She felt blessed even more when Isaac moved again, while she was pressed against me, and both of us could feel him move. We both burst out laughing and we went out beyond our ring of tents and made a thank offering to El Shaddai. Cakes and oil. I was so thrilled with this new experience of life that I did not think killing an animal was the right response.

Our household was doing well, and I had plenty to eat. I made sure to drink plenty of good water, with no adverse commentary from Abi. The most miraculous pregnancy, anticipated for decades, announced by messengers from God . . . and the pregnancy and birth turned out to be normal? Ordinary, even? I had seen so many pregnancies and births, always aware that even though women have given birth every day since time immemorial, this ordinary event was always miraculous. You see a birth and you know something about God, whatever else you may believe about that God or gods in general. And there I was, suspended between ordinary and miracle.

It was a routine delivery, midwifed by Ta-Sherit and a few of the other experienced women in our camp, including my old friend Jokim, for whom I had midwifed many times. Plenty of women wanted to be in on an important event like the birth of a child of Abraham, just like they had been when Ishmael was born. Ta-Sherit was gaining in proficiency, and she was the one I wanted with me. Ta-Sherit had become interested in midwifery ever since I told her of the prophecy about Ishmael having twelve sons. Her coming of age had ushered in a period of rebellious and disrespectful behavior, which I must admit is not unusual at that age. I tried not to remember how Merai and I had behaved at that age. Despite her know-it-all attitude, she simultaneously could be remarkably vacant about learning anything from me during those years, even though she had been a bright little girl. But motherhood and her encounter with the angel of God had matured her and she was a good mother to Ishmael. Then, once she realized how she would benefit from knowing about midwifery, she acknowledged she would find no better teacher of the lore of pregnancy and childbirth than me. I was delighted that my girl wanted to learn. And I felt vindicated that she considered me to be an expert.

I was also relieved on a practical level: it was good for her to have a special skill. Her place in our household was in many ways precarious. She had risen in status by becoming Abi's second wife. Our people associated her with me, but by seeing her as my servant. Ta-Sherit consoled herself with the conceit that she was the daughter of the Egyptian Pharaoh, but everyone else in our camp saw her as fatherless, and hence a non-entity, until she married Abi. It wasn't hard to figure out that she would likely outlive both Abi and me, and what would be her place then? If she learned the skill of delivering babies, I thought, she might be respected and be able to make her way in the world. Fortunately, my girl was as smart as she was beautiful, and she learned all that I had to teach her. Which was quite a lot.

But, back to the subject of that delivery: my miraculous son Isaac. There he was, at last, at last, at last! My womb was good enough. All my married life, I had wondered about that, and wondered why God had not opened it. Ever since my time in the harem in Egypt, I wondered if I had ruined it, or if it had rotted with my old age, but the birth of Isaac assured me my womb was good enough. Praise God. At last. Good enough.

When the afterbirth came out, intact and looking just like a normal afterbirth, which is to say, ugly, I felt as though all my sins had been removed, painfully but completely. When I was able, Ta-Sherit helped me walk outside and we buried the afterbirth. I'd seen that done after some births I had midwifed in other places Abi and I had travelled through. The custom, as far as I understood it, seemed to have something to do with ensuring that the child would always be connected to that land. It seemed an auspicious thing to do. God had spoken to us of land and descendants, so it felt right to connect Isaac to this land.

I wrapped Isaac in that little part of a blanket I had started to weave in Pharaoh's harem but cut off the loom unfinished when Abi arrived to take me back. The blanket always reminded me that change can happen. I was at last holding my baby son, the change I'd spent my whole life wanting.

Abi was thrilled at the birth, of course, and would have been willing to sacrifice every animal we owned as a thank offering if God had asked for it. But God did not ask for it, and Damascan Eliezer kept Abi on the prudent side of ecstasy regarding the thank offering.

And then: the nursing. My ancient breasts still worked. Is anything impossible for God Almighty? Thank you, El Shaddai, God of mountains, God of breasts! The pins and needles tingling, which I still remembered from so many years ago in the harem in Egypt, was like a blessing. My milk flowed and my tears flowed with it. Baby Ta. And at last, a baby of my own.

Leaving

Chapter 18

THE NEXT FEW YEARS passed in a slow blur. It was a time filled with the ordinariness of life in Canaan. Planting, harvesting, this crop, that crop. Moving the flocks and herds, shearing the sheep, looking for pasture, looking for water. And for me, caring for precious Isaac. No cataclysmic interruptions scarred our lives, like spending years in a foreign harem. No instructions or promises from God. No visitations from heavenly messengers showing up with commands or promises or mysteriously knowing the unspoken thoughts in our hearts. The absence of communication from God sometimes felt troubling. God had come through with Isaac. What next? A great nation? Land? When? Were we running out of time?

Most of the time, I was so wrapped up with taking care of Isaac's day-to-day needs that I was too occupied or exhausted to think about the big picture of what God had in mind for us. God blessed us with prosperity, and I had plenty to eat as I nursed Isaac. I was so hungry! It must be awful to have to breastfeed during a famine. Once he started sleeping through the night and I wasn't so achingly tired all the time, I noticed that Ishmael did not get along with other people. Ta-Sherit tried to smooth things over between him and others. Ta-Sherit helped me with Isaac, of course. We were still close and I continued to teach her about delivering babies, along with all the care of the mother that should occur before and after the big event. She spent nights in her own tent, and Abi slept in his tent. And, yes, I would know. He and I were as close as ever, fascinated by every little thing our Isaac did.

"What kind of tree will he be?" quipped Abi. "A cedar or a palm?"

"Or maybe an oak or a tamarisk?" I replied. "He is his own little person."

Five years of age is the usual time to wean, and I reveled in motherhood so much that I was happy to keep nursing him a couple times a day, even though of course he was eating regular food as well. I was fortunate that there were no food shortages and that I did not have to do a lot of hard physical work during those years. It was a great blessing to be able to devote my time and energy to mothering this miraculous baby God had promised to my husband and me so long ago. Oh, please, please, please don't let this be the last time I ever nurse a baby, I prayed when I finally nursed Isaac for the last time. I was ready to have another baby, to keep working towards that great nation of our descendants.

The house of Abraham had a big feast to celebrate the weaning of Isaac. Weaning is worthy of a celebration. So many children die before their fifth birthday. Anyone can die at any age, of course, but if you can make it to five years, your outlook for a reasonable lifespan is good. Damascan Eliezer pointed out something else about reaching the age of five: that is about when the amount of food you can produce becomes greater than the amount of food you consume. Oh, that Eliezer, always thinking in terms of household economy. And it's a good thing he does, as that is not Abi's best skill.

Ishmael had been a typical boy, mischievous and active, but adolescence hit him hard. The circumcision at age thirteen certainly didn't help. It's hard to tell if that's what started the troubles, or if it just made an existing situation worse. He was behaving in the rebellious way typical for his age, and then his father cut him like that. Ta-Sherit had been horrified and tried to stop Abraham. She hadn't been included in the revelation about circumcision, like I was. She must have heard of Abraham's announcement to the men of our camp, but perhaps she only heard it second- or third-hand, and without the part about God's command.

She grabbed Abi's arm that was holding the knife and tried to stop him. That caused a rift between the two of them from which they never recovered. Abi knew he was doing what God commanded and resented her interference. Ta-Sherit knew about God but not about that particular command, and couldn't understand why Abi was doing something she saw as violent and bizarre. I knew that Egyptians practiced circumcision—remember, I do have reason to know this—but Ta-Sherit was still a little girl when we left Egypt and there had never been any reason for her to know about this custom among the Egyptians.

Ish withdrew emotionally from his father, even though Abi continued to be ever so fond of him. I had done a reasonably good job of fulfilling my vow to step back from raising Ishmael during boyhood. So, by the time he reached manhood, I had very little influence or authority over him. Ish just became wilder and wilder. Ta-Sherit was the only one who could get through to him, but less and less often. Some people in our household thought the problem was that he had been spoiled, that the long-awaited son of Abraham thought he deserved the special and indulgent treatment he'd received all his life, including from me, I have to admit, and could get away with doing whatever he wanted. "Living in conflict with all his relatives," the prophecy had said. Yes, indeed. That was Ishmael.

We all knew that Ishmael was a difficult, rebellious young man. We wanted to sweep the prophecy about being "a wild donkey of a man" under the rug because that was not what we wanted for our boy. In Ishmael, I could see Hakkin revived and multiplied—of course, I was the only one who knew that Hakkin was Ishmael's grandfather. I could see in Ishmael all Hakkin's least attractive traits, and there were plenty of them. It astounded me to think of the differences between Hakkin and Terah. I marveled that they could both be his grandfathers, and that two such different men could be connected to each other in any way, let alone by being the grandfathers of the same child.

From time to time, the herders found some of our animals dead from unknown causes. The animals had not been sick, and they bore no marks of injuries. This continued for months, and the whole camp grew uneasy about it. Was this a message or warning from our God? Had we done something to displease God? Was this a plague sent upon our household? We owned so many animals that no one was going hungry because of these mysterious losses. But if we lost too many animals, we would lose our livelihood. I was preoccupied with taking care of Isaac and therefore did not focus on the flocks and herds, other than being baffled and worried about the situation like everyone else. Our steward, Damascan Eliezer, was a good manager: smart, strict, and unyielding, but diplomatic. This was a problem for him to solve, not me.

One evening, Damascan Eliezer came to Abi in his tent while I was there. "Master Abraham, I've been trying to get to the bottom of this mystery of the dead animals. I've been watching each herd and each flock, watching the herders do their work, while keeping myself hidden," he said.

"I've been doing this for weeks and at last I have the answer. Today I saw Ishmael strangle a calf with his bare hands."

"What? Why? Was the calf attacking him?"

"No. He seemed to do it just for the fun of it. Of course, there are many situations where we kill animals for food or sacrifices. But the killing of animals must not be taken lightly. He laughed at the calf as it struggled. After it was dead, he played with it and flapped its legs and head around. I could hear him laughing and talking to it, but I was too far away to make out his words. Then he just walked away and left the carcass there to rot in the sun."

Ishmael was physically capable of this; he had the strong hands of an archer. It takes a great deal of strength in one's hands to string a bow, nock an arrow and shoot. As a skilled archer, he was used to killing animals. The house of Abraham had been quite prosperous all of Ishmael's life—of course, some years were better than others—and Ishmael had never known want. He had never developed the respect for food that one develops by living through a famine.

Abi, Eliezer, and I, along with most of our household, had experienced famine several times in our lives and abhorred the waste of food. "It is an ungrateful response to our blessings of plenty, to waste assets this way, killing livestock for the fun of it," Eliezer continued. "How will El Shaddai react to this waste and insolence?"

"I do not believe Ishmael did this," said Abi.

"I am speaking the truth. I have seen it with my own eyes. Master Abraham, surely you must understand that we cannot have a man like that as part of our household. He kills animals and no one can control him. No one can even get along with him. He quarrels with all our workers and has assaulted many of them. Where will this lead if he is not stopped? He is arrogant; he does not control his anger and his next act could be to kill someone. He is on course to destroy the household."

Abraham stared at him.

"I'm sure you understand that a person who behaves like Ishmael cannot live with us." Receiving no response from Abraham, he paused before going on. "Do you remember that tribe we sojourned with for a while, after we left Egypt but before settling in Canaan? They had a harsh rule for how to deal with an incorrigible son. The father and mother of a son who would not obey them brought him to the elders of the community and testified that the son is stubborn and rebellious. And then the men of the community stoned him to death. I am not saying that Ishmael should be stoned or otherwise put to death. I am not saying that at all. It is a strange law. But it shows that the community has a role in stopping unacceptable behavior and that parents have responsibilities to the well-being of the community."

I don't think Abi heard any of that. He repeated that he did not believe Eliezer and stormed out of the tent.

That left me with Eliezer, who turned to me. "Please, Mistress Sarah, will you watch Ishmael without letting him know what you are doing? See if you see him doing the same. If you see Ishmael playing around like this, your corroboration will help Master Abraham face the facts and do what needs to be done to protect our household's livelihood."

A curious line of thought, it seemed to me. Was Eliezer trying to get Ishmael disinherited, without looking like he had done so? I had known Eliezer all his life—he had been born in our household—and I had long had the greatest respect for his trustworthiness and managerial abilities. But then there was the harassment of Ta-Sherit. That dimmed my opinion of him. I know that men with power often consider themselves entitled to sexual favors from women who are easy prey. And I didn't need to spend years in Pharaoh's harem to figure that one out. What he did to Ta-Sherit wasn't surprising, just disappointing. Also, it happened without my knowledge—and I would like to think that I am not in the habit of missing things. What else was going on in Eliezer's heart that I didn't know about?

And look at what Ta-Sherit had done with that situation, leveraging the one advantage she had, a relationship with me, into a huge elevation in status for herself. Was Eliezer trying to get back at her for that, by having her son sent away, or worse? If he succeeded, Ishmael would not inherit along with Isaac. I wondered if Eliezer's next move would be to figure out a way to get rid of Isaac or otherwise have him disinherited, a thought that made my blood run cold. Might he also try to get rid of any other sons that I or Ta-Sherit might have? Even if I was the only human who had hopes of my having another child, it was entirely reasonable to think that Ta-Sherit could have more sons. The angel of El Shaddai at Beer-lahai-roi told her she would have a huge, uncountable number of descendants. That didn't necessarily mean only through Ishmael and his twelve princes. Eliezer knew every word of that prophecy. Maybe he would try to get her sent away with Ishmael, even though the problem was all about Ishmael.

I refused his request to spy on Ishmael, left Abi's tent and went to find him and console him.

But in a couple of days, Eliezer got his wish. Without expecting to, I did see Ishmael and I reported what I had witnessed to my husband. I didn't want to, but I couldn't not do it.

"Abi, I have to tell you something."

"You look disturbed. What is it?"

"I am disturbed. Very early this morning, I was walking to the well to draw water. Hardly anyone was around. I've been waking up early, unable to fall back asleep."

"One of the many burdens of old age."

"That's for sure. So, I figured I might as well get going and draw water while it was still cool and while I still had the energy to do so. On the way, I saw a dead sheep. I looked around and saw Ishmael at a distance. He was strangling another sheep. When Eliezer first told you and me about seeing Ishmael strangling a calf, I wondered if Ishmael was doing this as some misguided idea of how to make a sacrifice. But now that I've seen it myself, I could see it was not. He laughed at that poor sheep's struggle, and then he played with the dead body before leaving it lying on the ground."

Abi was silent.

"We have to admit that Eliezer was right," I said.

A long pause. Then, "Yes. The fact that you have seen it yourself matters."

Chapter 19

ABI WAS VERY UPSET about the whole situation. He was disappointed in the son he loved so much. Everyone, including a reluctant Abi, agreed that Ishmael would have to go away. You simply cannot have someone like that around if you make your living by herding. The servants, the entire household, were all of one opinion. The substance of Eliezer's accusation and his plea to Abi became generally known throughout the camp. Ishmael had no friends among them—his hand had been against every one of them at some time or another, and in turn, all hands were against him.

I went to talk to Ta-Sherit. "I understand, he can't stay as part of our household," she said, looking hurt and embarrassed. "I heard the angel's prophecy myself and I know better than anyone who and what Ishmael is."

The only question was, should we send Ishmael out alone, or should Ta-Sherit go with him? Everyone perceived me as being in charge of her, so I was the one who was expected to make the decision. I loved my girl. I would see flashes of my friend Bee-bee in her, which warmed my heart. Remembering Bee-bee reminded me: Bee-bee's parents had sold her into slavery. Bee-bee gave Ta-Sherit away as soon as she had the chance. I wanted the mother to stay with her child, for once, in this generation of her family. So, on the one hand I wanted her to go with Ishmael, but on the other hand, I didn't want to lose her. It was hard to think of losing her. But Abraham was giving up his son, so how could I refuse to give up my girl?

Just because everyone else thought I was the one to make the decision about her didn't mean I saw it that way. "Ta-Ta, do you want to stay with us or go with Ishmael?"

"I accept that Ishmael must leave. And I know all the prophecies you and Abraham and I have received about descendants and about Ishmael and Isaac in particular. I know that Isaac, not Ishmael, will be the one to inherit the covenant that El Shaddai made with Abraham."

"We don't really know what that means about the covenant. But one thing we do know is that it's about Isaac and his descendants. And we know that Ishmael has his own blessing from El Shaddai," I said.

"If I go with Ishmael, maybe I can get him set up with a wife and a father-in-law who will give him an honest livelihood."

"Unfortunately, I don't think Ish will do too well on that score, left to his own devices."

She chose to go. "Daughters leave," she said quietly. "That's the way it works."

I had to recognize that she was ready to leave home. She was a grown woman, the mother of a teenage son whom she loved and wanted to keep out of trouble. The mother-son bond is strong. And I knew that she still felt the pull of Egypt, and that she still was considered a foreigner, still referred to as "Ha Gaaar" by most of our household. She was closely associated with me, the first wife of the patriarch, but I was old and getting older. I could offer her security while I was alive, but not much of anything afterward. Same for Abi. What would be her status as a widow with no son? Not an enviable situation for any woman to be in.

I went to Abi and said Ta-Sherit should go out with her son, and reminded him that God previously had told us that her son Ishmael would not inherit the covenant along with my son Isaac. Abi still wasn't keen on sending Ishmael away. He said he would ask El Shaddai for guidance, and prayed that he would receive instructions in a dream. Those instructions did come, promptly and clearly: "Whatever Sarah tells you, do as she says." Thank you, El Shaddai! Affirmation like that from a god, any god, doesn't happen every day. That pronouncement from El Shaddai was emphatic enough that it was always retold and then written down as part of our family's history. But some people prefer their own opinion to God's and think I did wrong. I said what I said, and that's what we did, with our God's endorsement.

Once Ta-Sherit told me of her decision, a few days passed while plans were made for their departure. Ta-Sherit would go to Egypt with Ishmael. But the first stop would be to visit Lot and his family. Abi and I talked to Ta-Sherit and Ishmael (to the extent he would listen) about what to do. Ishmael stood by, silent and sullen.

"You remember Cousin Lot, right?"

"Yes," said Ta-Sherit. "He was always kind to me. I remember he was the one who first explained to me the difference between a sheep and a goat, way back when we left the house of Pharaoh."

"Can you believe you once didn't know that?"

"It's been a long time," Ta-Sherit continued. "His wife Adoth is Egyptian, like me. I always liked her. I wonder if she has ever gone back to Egypt? Maybe she can tell me about it before we go there." Ta-Sherit was getting excited about the prospect of Egypt. "Do you think I can find my birth mother at the palace? Do you think my father Pharaoh will remember me?"

"I don't think it would be a good idea to go there. Especially if you show up saying you are Pharaoh's daughter. They will think you are there to cause trouble. I'd stay out of Thebes altogether if I were you." I wondered if Bee-bee was still alive. She no doubt would have become pregnant again and if she underwent another birth where she lost as much blood as the first one . . .

I was glad of a chance to spend some time with Ta-Sherit, having a long goodbye. I had not even had time to say the word "goodbye" to Bee-bee.

We sang my epic encyclopedia of pregnancy and birth together one more time. I wanted her to have the benefit of all I had learned in my long experience as a midwife. "Ishmael is going to get married and have a lot of children," she reminded me proudly. "A great nation. Twelve princes! I am going to need to know about delivering babies."

"You're going to be a wonderful grandmother, Ta." I had a momentary pang of feeling my age. I was the mother of a young boy and I wondered if I would live to see grandchildren. But I did not want to trouble her with my thoughts. I wanted her to get a good night's sleep before starting her journey. Before we went to bed, I retrieved the pouch of silver that King Abimelech of Gerar had given to Abi and sewed all the pieces of silver into inside pockets in Ta-Sherit's robe. Keeping money in a money pouch makes it too easy to be robbed of everything all at once. I kept the empty pouch as a memento of what she had done for me at the house of the King of Gerar.

We lay down on the sleeping mat in my tent together, curled up spoon-style, for the last time. My last night with Merai, the night before she was married, I knew it would be the last. My last night with Bee-bee, I did not know it would be the last. This time, with Ta-Sherit, the baby I didn't have, I knew this was the last night I would feel her luxuriant hair against my face and smell her skin while falling asleep. Surely Merai must be dead by now, I thought. Bee-bee, probably, but who knows? There was only Ta-Sherit, and, as she said, daughters leave.

Chapter 20

IT WAS ABRAHAM'S IDEA that they should first go to stay with Lot and his family in Zoar, where they went when they fled from the destruction of Sodom. By then, we had moved to the eastern part of the Negev, and Zoar was less than a day's journey away. Abi was always loyal to Lot and had undertaken quite some risk by arguing with God: Abi did not know what might happen if one argued with God. He talked God into promising not to destroy the entire city of Sodom, where Lot and his family lived at that time, if there were merely ten righteous people in it. Apparently, there weren't even ten good people in that whole city, though. One morning, Abi went back to the place where he had bargained with God and looked down towards Sodom and Gomorrah and the plain around them. He saw thick black smoke pouring up from the whole area. It was way too dangerous-looking for Abi or any of our men to go down there and investigate.

The first chance he got, Abi spoke to travelers who had passed through that area and questioned them about Lot's well-being. Abi was greatly relieved when the travelers told him that Lot and his family had made it out alive from Sodom and were living in Zoar. That made sense; Lot had always been attracted to Zoar. He had his eye on it even way back when he and Abi had separated. We did not know, then, that his wife and the men who were engaged to marry his two daughters did not make it to Zoar along with Lot and the daughters.

We did have some scruples about sending a young man whom we knew to be difficult to get along with to stay with our relatives. But we knew that Ishmael and Ta-Sherit would not stay long. Ta-Sherit intended to move southwest and settle in Egypt, and we expected that Ishmael would not want to stay in Zoar and adapt to city life.

"Lot is known to be a very gracious host," said Abraham. "And surely after all I've done for him over the years, he will take care of my son for a time and send the two of them on well-provisioned."

"And on the topic of provisions: what will we send them off with?" I asked.

"They just need enough food and water to get to Lot in Zoar. That is not far; they will start early in the morning and can get there the same day. God said Isaac is the one who is supposed to inherit. So, I am not supposed to divide the property. I do not want to anger God by disobeying instructions, especially when we want God's good favor for my son on this journey. Lot can give them as much as he wants; God did not say anything against that. Surely my nephew will be a good host and be generous to my son." I could understand Abi's not wanting to anger God, considering what had happened to Sodom and Gomorrah.

Abraham got up early in the morning, which was a good thing, because Ishmael had gotten up even earlier. He had just started off alone, carrying the bundle of food and skins of water that had been set out the evening before for him and Ta-Sherit to take with them. Abi called him back; Ishmael sullenly complied. Abi realized he had better make sure Ta-Sherit was carrying at least some provisions herself in case Ishmael ran ahead and she became separated from him. So, Abi took some bread and a skin of water and gave them to Ta-Sherit, putting them on her shoulder. He also placed Ishmael's hand on her shoulder and told him to stay with his mother.

"When you ran out on your family when you left Haran, you didn't take your mother with you." It's painful how disrespectful Ishmael could be to his father.

"That was different. I was married, and I took my wife," Abi said in a conciliatory tone. Why does he even bother to respond, I wondered.

"Oh right, you brought her along as part of the baggage so you could have sons. Since having sons is so important to you."

I could see this conversation was turning into something I did not want as a parting memory, so I stepped away with Ta-Sherit. She gave me a sly smile and opened the neck of her robe to show me she was wearing the gold necklace Pharaoh had given me and I had given her as a wedding gift. "Back to Egypt!" she said happily. We hugged each other for a long time before rejoining the group that had gathered to say goodbye.

We sent them off with songs, the women played their timbrels, and our best musician played a lyre (very fancy!) that he had recently acquired.

Ta-Sherit and Ishmael set out from our camp, and they turned their faces towards Zoar. Abraham and I went with them for a little distance to set them on their way. And off they went to stay with Lot in Zoar.

Just one problem: Lot no longer lived in Zoar.

Chapter 21

IT WAS ONLY MUCH later that we learned about Lot and his daughters leaving Zoar, and the rest of that sordid story. Spice traders from the south who had passed through Zoar told us about it. They started with the part we already knew: the horrifying destruction of Sodom by God as retribution for the lack of hospitality the men of Sodom inflicted on the two of our mysterious three visitors who traveled on to that city. The traders also had heard that Lot's wife and the two men living in Lot's house who were engaged to marry the daughters did not escape Sodom. Only Lot and his two daughters made it to Zoar. And then they told us more of the story, further information that was news to us: the family left Zoar—the traders did not know why—and Lot found a cave up in the hills for the three of them to live in. I could easily imagine him doing that: Lot had lived so much of his life on the move, following the flocks, living outside or in tents. He was well suited to it. I could also easily imagine Adoth giving up, stopping, and crying when they fled Sodom.

But what they said about Lot and Adoth's two daughters left me unsettled. The traders told us that Paltith and Thamma became hysterical and thought there were no men left in all the world except their father. That did not sound likely: their mother is from Egypt, their father is from Ur, by way of Haran, they'd lived in Sodom and they'd lived in Zoar. Surely, they knew the world is a big place. Yet somehow, even with Sodom destroyed, they thought there were no men left in the entire world except their father?

The next thing the traders told us was even more troubling. The story they had heard was that the daughters, thinking there were no men left in the world except their own old father, concluded that they must have sex with him so they could each get pregnant and provide him with male descendants. And so, they got him drunk with wine, so drunk that he did not know what he was doing, and on consecutive nights each of them seduced him, and became pregnant by him. Each daughter bore Lot a son: the older daughter's son was named Moab and the younger daughter's son was named Ben-ammi.

Abi was dismayed that Lot's daughters would do such a thing. I was dismayed that Abi accepted this story without skepticism. I've heard stories of incest. One can hear a lot of stories about women's lives while sitting for hours with other women, waiting for a baby to come. I have never heard of a young marriageable woman seducing a male relative who was decades older than herself. Never. That is not the way incest happens. I have always heard about it being instigated by the older or more powerful man. The man might be drunk, but not because the younger woman intentionally got him drunk. More likely, the man got the younger woman drunk. I was overwhelmed with grief and disgust over Lot's behavior.

Lot lost his house and everything in it when Sodom was destroyed. We never found out what happened to him in Zoar, but he was unable to prosper there. He had lost so much and it seems he had lost his good sense, too. He kept living in the cave in the hills, away from people. What demon had gotten into him? It seems he had forgotten about El Shaddai, even though angels had come to him, stayed in his house, and told him how to save himself and his family. Most people don't get help like that, no matter how much they sacrifice and pray. You would think it would make a person's connection to El Shaddai unshakable.

Lot knew about El Shaddai. He knew why Abi left his father, brother, and the rest of their family in Haran, and Lot chose to come with us. I know that he told his wife, Adoth, about our God. And she seemed willing to accept an additional god. But she was Egyptian and she may have been unwilling to completely let go of her ancestral gods. The daughters must have heard of El Shaddai from their father, but I have no idea how much they understood about El Shaddai's power. Well, no doubt they had a better idea after the destruction of their city. The men to whom they were engaged obviously did not understand at all. They thought Lot was joking when he told them his God was about to destroy Sodom! Good riddance to those two donkeys! But what about the daughters? Abi's great-nieces. Terah's great-granddaughters. And look what had happened: each of them was the mother of a son fathered by her own father. Neither girl was what one would hope for in a descendant of Terah.

Ultimately, neither was Lot. Despite all the care that his grandfather Terah and his uncle Abi had poured into him, he wound up a broken vessel. Lot still owned land east of the Jordan and the Dead Sea. That is where his sons/grandsons eventually settled. Neither of them became what they could have been. What a disappointment. Again I tried, unsuccessfully, to figure out the interaction between God's will and human action.

But enough of that. The point is, when Ta-Sherit and Ishmael arrived in Zoar to find cousin Lot, he was no longer there and no one knew where he was. His previous city of residence, Sodom, was just a smoking hole in the ground, so no help there, either. Ta-Sherit and Ishmael turned south through the desert towards Egypt and kept going.

By the time we found out what had happened and where Lot's cave was, Ta-Sherit and Ishmael were long gone. It was an even longer time before we learned that they had run out of water as they journeyed in the desert—it seems like the people of Zoar are not much more hospitable than the people of Sodom—and how God heard Ishmael's voice and spoke to Ta-Sherit, showed her a well, and saved them. In addition to the obvious physical relief of finding water, for Ta-Sherit it was a huge relief to have her faith in El Shaddai confirmed, to know that El Shaddai was still with her, so far from home, and repeating the promise that Ishmael would father a great nation. I only found out about it years after it happened, but even at that late date, I felt overwhelmed with pride in Ta-Sherit. She received a second visitation from God. My girl is important to El Shaddai.

Now I Know

Chapter 22

But I am getting ahead of myself. We found out about all that many years later. Meanwhile, I had a darling little boy to raise. And that is what I did, for many years.

We loved Isaac! Have any parents in the history of the world been so focused on their child? We cherished our wonderful, miraculous boy and told him about El Shaddai, starting when he was too young to understand our words. That way, he would feel that he had always known of El Shaddai, and not be aware of a time before he had first heard of him. He was a sweet-tempered little boy. Sweet like Abi. He stayed with me in my tent maybe a little longer than is customary for a son, because we got along together so well. He certainly didn't give me the behavior and discipline problems that Ishmael had given Ta-Sherit.

Ishmael got along with Isaac—at least as well as Ishmael got along with anyone. Isaac, for his part, was unaware of his older brother's difficulties with other people. Isaac admired Ishmael, and he wanted to be a great bowman like Ishmael when he grew up. He liked to eat the game that Ishmael hunted because he liked the taste of it better than what he called the "daddy meat" from our flocks and herds. Abi just laughed when he heard about this. He wanted his sons to get along and never gave up on that hope, even after it became clear that Ishmael was not good at getting along with anyone.

Abi frequently prayed that they would be good brothers to each other and continued to do so even after Ishmael left us. "It's so good, so pleasant, for brothers to live in harmony!" he said frequently. Unfortunately, brothers living in harmony does not happen all that often. Even so, I still wished for more sons and hoped they would be the exception and dwell together in harmony.

God had spoken of Abi's descendants as "a great nation," Abi was sure of it. He was sure that was what God had promised him, so long ago in Haran. That promise of many descendants had been repeated, to both of us. After we escaped from Egypt and Lot went his own way, God told us that we and our descendants, who would be uncountable like the dust of the earth, would be given the length and breadth of the land.

That message had come to us yet again near Mamre's oaks at Hebron, still my favorite place in all the world. Our wanderings took us through there many times, and we always visited with Mamre, Eschol, and Aner and their families and talked about old times. I also prayed to and meditated on El Shaddai at the altar Abi and I had built there. I always had a good feeling at Hebron. God said our descendants would be uncountable. Uncountable! For me, at least, that raised the question of, "Uncountable by whom?" I was reminded of Bee-bee, who, I believe, could not count past twenty.

The "uncountable" promise had been further explained when Abi heard from El Shaddai at Hebron. His descendants would be as uncountable as the stars. As the stars! Hearing from El Shaddai was always a big event, but that occasion was particularly intense because it was a vision in which they had a conversation. It was rare for Abi to be able to ask questions. That was when Abi was told that his own issue would be heir, which is to say, not Damascan Eliezer. So far as I know, Abi never told Damascan Eliezer that El Shaddai said that. I know I didn't tell him. When Abi had that vision and conversation, neither Ishmael nor Isaac had been born.

Abi and I already had one son. That was a start. Again, as before, nothing was happening in the way of producing babies. By then, I was no longer controlled by the two-week/two-week pattern. The Isaac pregnancy was a miracle, and miracles can happen on any day of the month. But it did not happen on any day. Abi and I prayed together, separately, silently, out loud, at home in the tents, out in the fields, at altars. We wanted instructions and even more, we wanted results.

We were living in the desert of Beer-sheba when Abi received another message. He told me about it immediately, of course. He was shaking. After he told me, I was shaking, too. "He called my name, the new name he had given me, Abraham, and I said I was there for him, listening to him," Abi began. "He said, 'Take your son' and I thought, 'Which one?' and he said, 'Your only son,' and I thought, 'I have two,' and he said, 'Whom you love,' and I thought, 'I love them both,' and then he said, 'Isaac.'"

"Isaac. That's a roundabout way of identifying him. But clear, eventually," I mused.

"I have two sons and I love them both. Doesn't God know that? And then he said to take Isaac to the land of Moriah and offer him—Sarah, brace yourself for this—as a burnt offering on a mountain there; he would show me which one."

Stunned silence. Sacrifice Isaac? Can it be? Is this our God, or an imposter god? We had been praying for instructions, but these were instructions we did not want to follow. "It must be the right thing to do," Abi said, shaking his head. "This must be the thing to do to get a multitude. Do you remember a story they told in Ur? The drops of blood turning into men?" Of course, I had heard the story. But that story was from long, long ago. And I had heard a lot of stories.

We had not heard from our God for several years; the last time was when El Shaddai told Abi to do what I told him about Ta-Sherit and Ishmael. El Shaddai told him that descendants would be named for Abi through Isaac. So, based on the most recent communication, we knew that Isaac was the key to the fulfillment of the promise of a multitude of descendants.

"We must figure this out," I insisted. "Is this our God talking? Is this something El-Shaddai would want you to do? Let's think this through and consider everything we have heard from our God and determine whether this is the kind of request God would make. We must not make a mistake about this."

"We have only heard from El Shaddai a few times, now that I think of it," said Abi. "It seems as though it has been more often because each instance is so momentous that it reverberates in my heart for years. The first time was back in Haran, when I was told to leave my father's house and go to a land El Shaddai would show me. That was hard. It was against expectations that a son would leave his father like that, and kind of crazy that I should give up so much property that I would have inherited along with my brother Nahor."

"But it worked out well! You did lose your inheritance from Terah by leaving. I must admit I was worried about that at the time, since we did not know where we were going or what we would find there. But now you are even richer than your whole family was when we were in Haran."

"Yes. We have heard that Nahor has prospered, but I have done at least as well. And I would have only a third of what Nahor has now, so yes, it turned out better to take the risk and go as instructed. I always suspected that El Shaddai had told my father the same thing about going to a land that he would show him when Father packed up our family and moved us from Ur. I never asked him about this. I think he was the one who was supposed to come to Canaan, but he only went as far as Haran and then stopped."

"I never asked him either, but I think you are right. I think something inside of him broke. Father Terah just got stuck. Or maybe he thought that he did not have to do anything and he should just sit still and have faith that El Shaddai would get him to wherever he was supposed to be. Your father was a great man. I have always wondered why he stopped at Haran."

"Yes, I always thought it was supposed to be our whole family and that was why I wanted to bring Lot with us. I tried to get Nahor and Milcah to come, too, because it was supposed to be the whole family of Terah in the unknown land. I would still be happy for them and their children to come here and settle with us."

"Yes, well, that is a project for another day. We must focus and figure out this command about Isaac."

"The next time I heard from El Shaddai was at Shechem, near Moreh's oak trees. 'To your offspring I will give this land,'" Abi recalled.

"Words worth building an altar for, for sure!"

"But no commands, same as the next time, after Lot chose his own territory, 'I will give this land to you and your offspring, and will make your offspring uncountable.' The next time, God said my descendants would be as uncountable as the stars. But again, no commands."

"The next time any of our family received instructions from El Shaddai was Ta-Sherit at Beer-lahai-roi when the angel told her to return to me. That was exactly the opposite of what she wanted right then. But she did it and things worked out well. She gave birth to Ishmael safely and she and I became even closer after that."

"It's another example of instructions you don't want, but they turn out to be the right thing." Abi sighed. "That was also when she received the prophecy about what kind of man Ishmael would be. I wasn't happy to hear it and I wanted to think it must have been a mistake or that Ta-Sherit had misunderstood the angel. But it has been some comfort to me to know the prophecy about his character, to know that is the way he is, from before his birth, and there was nothing we could have done about what he is like."

"The next time we were told to do something was the big one, the one about covenant," I recalled. "Do you remember how ecstatic we felt, for days afterwards? El Shaddai said you would have a son by 'Sarah.' You fell on your face and laughed. I remember thinking, 'Was that what has been holding me back? Did I need to use the name 'Sarah' instead of 'Sarai' in order to have a son? If only I'd known that when we were first married.' And that message was specific about Isaac. El Shaddai said that I would have a son, what to name him, and that the covenant would continue through him. Ishmael would be the father of twelve princes, but the covenant would be established with Isaac. So, all the information in that most important message, which we both heard, emphasized the importance of Isaac. I simply do not know how to make sense of the command you just received in view of that earlier message. It's incomprehensible."

"I was thrilled when we heard that my beautiful wife would give rise to nations. But when I came down from my state of ecstasy, I had to face the unwelcome command that came with it. Do you remember the response I got when I made the announcement that all the men and boys in our household had to be circumcised? That is the most prominent example of God telling me to do something I did not want to do, something I could not justify doing, apart from it being a command from God."

"Horrifying. It did not make sense. It was bloody and painful. And yet, it was what God said to do. Some of the men ran away. No one died, that's the best I could say about it at the time." I had been more reluctant to circumcise Abi than I had been to do anything else in my life, except for when I had to defile myself with Pharaoh. I hoped never to see that miserable flint knife again.

"The next time God told me to do something, it was to do whatever you told me about Ishmael and Ta-Sherit."

"Ha! Well, that's not so bad, in my opinion! But let me tell you, I was thankful to El Shaddai for that confirmation. He must have known how ambivalent I was and how sad I was about losing my girl. Ta-Sherit had chosen to go with her son instead of staying with me. Once I conveyed that decision to you, I kept going back and forth in my heart as to whether I should overrule it, keep her with me, and send Ishmael out alone. But I had said what I said, and you had a command to do what I said."

"Yes, that was a difficult thing to do, for both of us. But it worked out well enough, eventually."

By then, we had heard that the two of them had settled in the wilderness of Paran, and Ta-Sherit had found an Egyptian wife for Ishmael. Ishmael and his wife had already started producing those promised twelve princes. My girl a grandmother already, and me still hoping for baby number two!

In addition to these messages, which were quite consistent about promising land and descendants, I reminded Abi of some other significant times when we saw how God acted in our lives. Back in Egypt, Abi had allowed me to be taken into Pharaoh's harem. Not good. But our God responded to Abi's bad move by plaguing Pharaoh, his household and land. Innocent Egyptians suffered and starved; Abi became richer. Abi recognized that he got better than he deserved, and we are both grateful for it. But neither of us understood the logic or justice of God's action in that situation.

Another time was when Abi bargained with God about the fate of Sodom. "I learned about God from that conversation, but it wasn't a matter of God giving me instructions, either easy or difficult instructions." Abi's face turned solemn. "It showed me his power. It showed me the importance of righteousness."

"And the importance of hospitality, specifically, in the case of the people of Sodom," I added.

"I have thought about what God told me about the number of our descendants. One time God said they would be as numerous as the dust of the earth. The next time, that they would be as uncountable as the stars. I do not see how one woman can have that many babies, even if there are twins or triplets. Even if a man has many wives having babies. And we know that is not the way because we know that they are all supposed to be through you, my dear Sarah. God must have some other way of providing a multitude." Abi sighed. "I believe this command truly is from El Shaddai. Even though it is horrifying and incomprehensible."

Our God was a surprising God. Our God had told us to do incomprehensible things. When we obeyed, it turned out to be the right thing to do; the situation had worked out well for us. Maybe not as quickly as we wanted, but eventually. El Shaddai promised absurd things, and then delivered on them. We had limited experience with how this God acts, and we did not know much about him . . . or her. We still did not even know that. We certainly did not understand the ways of this God of ours. And we had to face this horrifying instruction that seemed exactly contrary to God's promise of Isaac producing multitudes of descendants.

"Maybe this is the way. Make Isaac into multitudes by drops of his blood," Abi whispered, reluctant to voice this conjecture.

"That's absurd. That can't happen." And yet, I did like the idea of a multitude of Isaacs, all just like him, with his curly black hair and sweet disposition.

"The last time we doubted, we were told that nothing is impossible for God," Abi said, trying to sound confident.

"Last time, I only laughed to myself and the visitor knew what I was thinking. 'Is anything impossible for God Almighty?' he asked. That scared me. And the next thing you know, I'm pregnant."

"'Is anything impossible for God Almighty?' I have been saying that to myself over and over again, ever since."

"So have I." I shook my head and shrugged, while tears ran down my face. "Ours is a very unusual God."

"That is what we were supposed to learn. Nothing is impossible for God Almighty. We should not have doubted that you would become pregnant. I, too, laughed. Fell on my face and laughed. It was that time when El Shaddai told us about covenant and circumcision. He told us you would have a son. I thought it was so absurd I just asked for a blessing for Ishmael."

"Faith is hard."

"Faith is hard." Abi sighed and said, "It must be that when I cut Isaac the drops of blood will turn into more boys. That must be what God is talking about. I didn't like cutting him when I circumcised him, but it was what God wanted and was the right thing to do." He sighed again. "I should do it fast before I change my mind. Tomorrow morning. I will rise early. I submit to the will of God."

I sent out our best hunter, then made a special dinner of wild game stew for Isaac that night. Abi chose two of the young men and had them pack a great deal of food and supplies to be loaded on the donkeys in the morning. He expected that he would need two helpers to tend to all the donkeys carrying the supplies, because he would have a lot of people to feed and care for on the trip home.

Chapter 23

THEY LEFT EARLY THE next morning, earlier than I thought they would. I knew that Abi did not want to pause for even a moment, lest he reconsider his decision. Once he's in motion, he stays in motion. I had only a moment to see them off, and by the time I was back in my tent, I had second thoughts. Why hadn't I told Abi I was going, too? How could I not be there for this momentous event, whatever it was that was going to happen? I had to go, even though it was not going to be easy to get ready and go at that point.

I found Damascan Eliezer and told him what I wanted to do. "You're not going alone, Mistress Sarah," he said. "I'm going with you. And we're taking the camels. That is our only chance of catching up with them." Despite my attempts to speed preparations along, it took hours to gather and pack supplies and saddle the camels. It is a three-day trip from where we were camped to the land of Moriah, and that requires a lot of supplies, especially since Eliezer was solicitous of my comfort and packed more than the bare necessities.

"Is anything impossible for God Almighty?" These words kept running through my heart, as I dashed around, gathering food and supplies for the journey. Could Isaac be made into multitudes? What would that look like?

Abi and Isaac's group was already out of sight. But we knew which way to go to the land of Moriah, even if we, like Abi, did not know exactly which mountain we were headed for. Even if we could not completely catch up, I hoped we could at least be close enough to see what would happen on whichever mountain God showed to Abi.

From time to time, if we were up high overlooking a valley or plain, we could see Abi's group. They would have been able to see us, but since they didn't know we were coming, at that distance we would have just looked like a small camel caravan, indistinguishable from any other. We had another advantage in tracking them. One of the donkeys in their group was big and strong, but had a problematic digestive system, and let's just say it was unpleasantly easy to figure out where it had been.

On the third day, we saw them at the foot of a mountain, and we were about to come down an adjacent hill, so we had a good view of them. We saw Abraham and Isaac leave the group, going up the mountain, Isaac carrying the wood, while the young men and donkeys stayed behind. "We can catch up with the servants now," cried Eliezer, "even if we can't catch up with Master Abraham."

"No," I responded. "We will watch from this hill and see what happens. It will take too long to go down this hill and then up that one. We have a better chance of seeing them on the mountain from here than from down there." We were able to see Abraham build an altar, arrange the wood on it, and maneuver Isaac, like a sack of something, onto the top of the pile.

"What is Master Abraham doing? Why doesn't Isaac run away?" murmured Eliezer.

I could see Abi's arm extended. I knew that it held a knife, even though I couldn't see it. "That miserable flint knife," I thought to myself.

Eliezer and I heard an angel's voice. I can't describe what it sounds like. You know it when you hear it. Because of the distance, we could only make out some of the words. "Abraham . . . do not . . . do anything to him . . . now I know you fear God . . . your only son . . ." We saw Abi lower his arm, help Isaac off the altar, and remove some rope he must have tied him with. Then we saw him walk a few steps away and pull an animal—it looked like a ram—out of some dense shrubbery it was stuck in.

"Eliezer, did you notice that ram stuck there before?"

"No, Mistress Sarah, I did not."

Abi wrestled the ram onto the wood, sacrificed it, and a few moments later, we saw the wood catch fire. Eventually, the smoke from the burning animal wafted our way. It smelled like perfume. Eliezer and I inhaled, then looked at each other in confusion and amazement.

"What kind of animal smells like that?" he wondered out loud.

"No animal on earth." I answered.

Isaac had run halfway down the mountain at this point. Eliezer and I and the camels came down from our hill to the place where Abi had left the young men and donkeys. I slid off my camel, ran to Isaac and we clung to each other. When Abi arrived, eyes shining and skin glowing, he told me and Eliezer what had happened. He filled in the words Eliezer and I had only partly heard. When Abi recounted the angel's words, "Now I know that you fear God," I heard Isaac, still clinging to me, murmur, "Now I know something, too."

We headed back home. Isaac, Eliezer, and the young men gathered the donkeys and supplies, while Abi and I rode ahead on the camels. He and I were able to talk privately on the way about what had happened and not happened. No multitude of Isaacs springing up from his blood. Just the original one, still alive, uninjured although shaken. Abi told me of God's reiteration of the promise of descendants, as many as the stars in the sky and as the sand on the seashore. God also told him something new (and as usual, both marvelous and baffling): all people of the earth would be blessed because of our descendants. What was that all about?

"We are still learning about this God. I wonder why God referred to Isaac as 'your only son.' Has something happened to Ishmael that we don't know about? And why command you to do something and then tell you not to at the last moment?" I shook my head. It just didn't make sense.

"Why did this happen? What are we supposed to learn from this?" Abi still seemed to be in shock or in some transcendent state from the experience.

"Do what God says? Trust God? What do you think we were supposed to learn?" I asked him.

"God provides? On the way up the mountain, Isaac pointed out that we were taking wood and fire but no lamb with us. I told him God would provide the lamb for the burnt offering. I didn't know what I was talking about, but it turned out to be true. Then suddenly, there was the ram. One animal, when one was all that was needed."

"We are supposed to learn the meaning of 'enough,' and about the power of one," I concluded. "The adequacy of one. One God is enough. One son is enough. We thought we needed a multiplicity of sons. Now I know we don't. Most people think they need a multiplicity of gods. They don't. They just need the right one." I was astounded by what had happened, of course, but was not as overwhelmed as Abi, and thus I was able to think a bit more clearly.

We were both embarrassed by our incorrect expectations. We could only excuse ourselves with the defense that we were still getting to know El Shaddai. And that retort, "Is anything impossible for God Almighty?"

was still in our hearts. Although we later told the story of what had happened on Mount Moriah many times, we never again mentioned what we had originally expected to happen.

Chapter 24

NEVER MENTIONED IT, EXCEPT to Isaac, that is.

He found me in my tent after he arrived with Damascan Eliezer, the young men, and the donkeys. "Mother, why did Father try to kill me? Is he going to try to kill me again?" he blurted out angrily immediately upon entering. It had been a three-day journey for both returning groups, but the events on Mount Moriah still felt like they had just occurred.

"No, Yitzi, no. Your father loves you. He did this because El Shaddai commanded him to."

"If that's so, then he loves El Shaddai more than he loves me. And no, El Shaddai did not tell him to do that, he told him not to do it. I was there. I heard what the angel said."

"Your father loves you. I love you."

"You love Father more than you love me."

What to do with that one? "I love you both. In different ways. It's different. You can't say one more than the other. You'll understand when you are married and have children."

"I hope I live that long. You love your husband more. I hope I wind up with a wife who loves me more than she loves our son. At least you loved me enough to come with Damascan Eliezer to rescue me from Father. But fortunately, the angel got there first because you didn't get there fast enough."

I wondered what, if anything, Damascan Eliezer had told him on the way home. Or maybe Isaac drew this conclusion on his own. It certainly could have looked to him like we were coming to rescue him. It was hard for any of us to figure out what happened and why. Isaac and I were both too worked up to respond to each other's arguments logically. This conversation was so different from the one Abi and I had just a week ago when discussing our past experiences of God.

"God did tell him to do it. God was testing your father. God knows your father loves you. When God saw that your father was willing not to withhold you, God knew that your father feared God. Then he told him not to do it. You heard the angel say that last part."

"Oh right, 'willing not to withhold me,' that's a nice way to say 'willing to kill me.' Does Father fear me, or anything else but God? What kind of God asks for that, anyway? Does God care about me?"

"Yes, Yitzi, God cares about you. You are important to God. He is going to establish his covenant with you."

"And that's an agreement to do what? Sacrifice my own children if that's what God asks for? Slaughter an entire village if that's what God asks for? Or the entire city of Jericho or someplace like that?"

"We don't know exactly what the covenant . . . "

"And what about destroying cities? What kind of God does that? Ours does. And that's another thing. When Father found out about God wanting to destroy Sodom, Father took a risk and argued with God and tried to talk him out of it. You and he have told me that story many times. Did Father do that for me? Did he even try to talk God out of this command to kill me?"

I hadn't thought of that parallel. "Uh, no," I muttered.

"Why not? 'Shouldn't the judge of all the earth do what is just?' Father talked back to God and said that then! He was willing to stand up for a city full of strangers, wicked strangers, but he wasn't willing to stand up for me!"

I wish I had thought of that when Abi and I had our conversation about the command.

"If Father is so good at obeying God, he had better obey the part about not laying a hand on me or doing anything to me."

"Isaac, your father thought that obeying God's command was the way to turn you into multitudes. He thought each drop of blood would turn into another one of you. You know our God has promised us a multitude of descendants. Did you hear the angel say so again on Mount Moriah? 'As many as the stars in the sky and as the sand on the seashore.' He thought there would be more of you, not the end of you."

"Like some kind of ancient creation story people tell while sitting around the fire drinking? That's ridiculous."

Should I tell him I had thought so, too? Once again, the thought ran through my heart, "Is anything impossible for God Almighty?" I think people who have been asked that question by an angel have different ideas about what is ridiculous and what is possible, compared to people who have not been so rebuked. And Isaac is on the other side of that divide from me.

Having dismissed the "instant multitudes" idea, Isaac calmed down a bit. "At least now I know what you and Father mean about hearing God and smelling the scent of bright light." Then something else occurred to him: Ishmael. "When the angel stopped Father, it spoke of me as the only son. Has something happened to Ishmael that I don't know about?"

"That's a good question. El Shaddai used the same words when giving your father the original command. He had the same thought: he has two sons and he loves you both. The last we heard, Ishmael and Ta-Sherit were settled and doing well. But news travels slowly."

"I nearly died. Maybe Ishmael wasn't so lucky. Who knows what El Shaddai might do." He stormed off to his own tent.

Chapter 25

ONE. THE ADEQUACY OF one. This was a huge release for me. I now knew that I did not need to have any more children. One child was enough, just as one God was enough. I had completed my assigned mission by bearing Isaac. The great nation will arise in some other way that our God will accomplish. The rest of my life was free time, a bonus. A little prayer popped into my heart and I kept singing it over and over to myself: "Holy One, now you can dismiss your servant in peace because you have kept your promise." Peace. At last, I had attained peace. I still did not know the name of our God, but now thought of God as "Holy One" and that was name enough.

I felt very old then. Holy One had kept me alive for a long time to complete the mission, and now I knew I had completed it. Not much more time; not much more to do; might as well make the best of it. I wanted to live at Hebron, but Abi wanted to move on and stay most of the year at Beer-sheba. He was better attuned to living in the desert. I don't know how, but his body conserved water in a way that no one else's did, and he did not mind the dryness. Abi, too, seemed to have reached peace after the encounter on Mount Moriah, except for one minor irritation. His old flint knife, his favorite, went missing. "What could have happened to it? I know I brought it back from Mount Moriah."

I could not tolerate the dryness of desert living so well anymore. Isaac wasn't too keen on desert life, either. He was even less keen on traveling with his father, and seemed relieved when Abi left for Beer-sheba. Isaac stayed at Hebron with me and lived in my tent. I told him stories of Abi's and my life together, and about our relatives. I told him as much as I could about our God. I told him to expect to hear new things from Holy One. He especially liked to hear about Ta-Sherit's conversation with Holy One at Beer-lahai-roi, and he wanted to see the place someday. He wanted a vision and an annunciation too, and he thought Beer-lahai-roi was a likely place for that to happen. He noticed I was proud of Ta-Sherit for having received such a blessing, and he wanted that experience, too.

I tried to engage him in conversation about what had happened on Mount Moriah. He did not want to talk about it, and only did so grudgingly. He seemed much quieter, no matter what the topic, than he had been before. He was a bit more willing to talk about the angel who had stopped Abi and I listened carefully to his recollection of what the angel was like and how he perceived its presence. Every message or visitation that any of us received from Holy One, by any method, in any place, was fascinating to me. I impressed upon him the importance of his mission to do what Holy One wanted, that his life was important to our God's plan, even though his father and I still did not understand the details of the promises of land and descendants. I wasn't so sure I was going to live long enough to see him married and a father. So I talked to him about choosing a wife, that he should pray and let Holy One lead him to the right woman. I told him I would be honored for him and his wife to live in my tent when I was gone.

In addition to his frequent silences, there was another change in Isaac's behavior. He refused to offer animal sacrifices. He still ate meat; he still hunted game. But he only offered grain and oil as sacrifices to Holy One. Normally, those are the kind of offerings a person or family makes if they are too poor to afford an animal, and that certainly was not our situation. When his father instructed him to sacrifice an animal, Isaac just stared at him for a long time, saying nothing.

Abi lived with us for part of the year. He, too, talked to Isaac about El Shaddai, the promises and the covenant, which seemed to be very important even though we did not have a very good idea of what it meant. Abi and I still loved each other, but we knew we would not have any more children together and that the nature of our marriage had changed. Cedar? Palm? Maybe one can survive without the other, after all.

There was only one more thing I wanted to do before I died: see Ta-Sherit. I wanted to visit my girl and say goodbye to her. We knew that she had hoped to take Ishmael to Egypt. I hoped she wasn't disappointed by what she found there.

We had heard that she had found an Egyptian wife for Ishmael and that Ishmael had children. I was excited to see Ta-Sherit's grandchildren! Originally, I planned to go with just a few servants. But Isaac wanted to come. Both Isaac and I were still a bit troubled about the "your only son" phrase from our most recent encounters with Holy One, and wondered whether something had happened to Ishmael. Also, Isaac was old enough to be interested in seeing more of the world. Egypt was the most sophisticated culture, and the richest, because you could count on the regular flooding of the Nile to produce abundant crops. Isaac knew his father and I had gone there because of a famine in Canaan, and he, too, had seen a few dry, bad years. So, I could understand his wanting to come with me. His silences made me feel as though I was losing him, in a different way than I had lost so many people who had once been close to me, but a loss just the same. I did not want to refuse him if he wanted to do something with me. On the other hand, I would have preferred having nothing to distract me from my final reunion with Ta-Sherit.

We made inquiries of passing traders. "Oh yeah, that Ishmael guy. We see him sometimes. Him and his mother used to live in the wilderness of Paran. But not anymore."

"Are they in Egypt?"

"No. Not in Egypt. Across the Red Sea from there. They and their crew live near the coast, west Arabia. Got a couple of wives and a bunch of children. Doing pretty well. Mostly we trade with him for leather, cloth, and camel butter."

I wondered if Ishmael had made himself unwelcome in Paran and that was the reason for the move. Ta-Sherit may have intended to go to Egypt, but she didn't get there, or if she did, she didn't stay there. Just as well.

"Isaac, on this trip we are not going to Thebes or anywhere near it. We won't even get as far as the Nile. We are just going through a lot of desert, some of which is claimed by Egypt. But not the part of Egypt you imagine."

"That's okay, Mother. I'm still interested in seeing another part of the land. I still want to go on this trip with you."

I wasn't going to tell him no. I was reluctant to enter Pharaoh's territory, let alone get anywhere near the capital, or the palace. So, I was relieved to hear the news of Ta-Sherit's relocation.

Surely the fetus in the sand must have decomposed by now, I thought.

We packed up and headed south from Hebron and stopped at Beersheba to stay with Abi for a while before continuing. My dear, dear, Abi! There is so much we have been through. Each of us wanted to know if the other had heard further instructions from God, or learned more about him. No, neither of us.

At the last minute, Abi decided he wanted to come with us, which was not what I had in mind. I had intended this visit to be about me and Ta-Sherit. But I also realized that this was likely my last journey with Abi, after having spent so much of our lives together on the move. So, he chose a few more servants to accompany us. Fortunately, Damascan Eliezer was not among them. He would oversee running the camp while Abi was gone. They loaded up more pack animals. I still remember his first camels, although they were long gone.

Isaac seemed uncomfortable with the change in plans. "You're with me the whole time, right, Mother? I mean, I can go on a trip with Father if other people are there, too."

"I'm there with you, Yitzi."

Onward south and east. On the way, we stopped at the spring at Beer-lahai-roi and camped there for a few days, taking advantage of the spring to water the animals and refresh ourselves. I retold the story about what had happened there. Isaac was very impressed that the angel of El Shaddai had appeared there and had saved Ta-Sherit. "Will El Roi see me here?" he asked, using the name that Ta-Sherit had given our God when she saw the fiery-flame-eyed angel there.

One day when we were camped near Beer-lahai-roi, I saw fragments of flint in the spring. They looked like the same type of flint as Abi's old knife, pulverized to bits. So that's what the pounding noise early in the morning had been. Good for you, Isaac; you do what you need to do. After the group circumcision, I wished I would never have to see that knife again. And thanks to Isaac, now I won't.

Isaac was reluctant to leave Beer-lahai-roi; I think he was hoping Holy One would appear there again. He had heard, smelled, and felt the presence of the angel on Mount Moriah, of course, and hoped for more encounters with Holy One. I can easily imagine he had some questions to ask about why Holy One issued that horrifying command. We all had questions we would like to ask, even though we knew that asking questions and receiving clear answers was not the way these encounters usually go.

Chapter 26

WE FOUND TA-SHERIT AND Ishmael's family living on the coastal plain, between the Red Sea and the mountains. Trade routes ran through the area. The existence of these routes, even though you wouldn't exactly call them roads, made it easier for us to find our way. Traders passing through knew who Ishmael was, and their directions helped us locate his family. When we asked for him, I got the impression that his neighbors knew who he was but did not like him very much. "His hand against everyone, and everyone's hand against him," still.

Ta-Sherit and Ishmael's wives were doing a pretty good job of keeping him in line, at least at home. Ta-Sherit doted on the flock of little children, just as any grandmother would. I was relieved to see her settled, happy and fulfilled. As for Ishmael, he was pleased to see his father and, from the welcoming and respectful way that he treated me, I could see that Ta-Sherit had told him about how close she and I had been. He called me Mama Sa-Sa, just like Ta-Sherit did. The old aggressiveness was still there, but he had learned to direct it towards the challenges of making a living trading, farming, and raising livestock in a dry, inhospitable land. Age and responsibility for his growing household had smoothed out some of his rough edges. He was a fine host to Abi, Isaac, and me, and to our servants; he graciously received our gifts. His two oldest daughters, Mahalath and Basemath, were particularly impressed with the gold bracelets we gave them. And the little ones were happy to see the honey and almonds.

"Yitzi! Is that you? You are so grown up now, my man!" was his greeting to Isaac upon our arrival. "The last time I saw you, you were only this high!" Ishmael continued to play the role of a fond big brother, and I could see that he and Isaac were going to get along just fine.

After we spent a few days in their camp, the men went off on a journey. Abi, Ishmael, Isaac, and Ishmael's two oldest sons, Nebaioth and Kedar, took a trip to have a good time and do some hunting together. I noticed Isaac questioning Ishmael, Nebaioth and Kedar as to whether they were definitely going along and staying for the whole journey. They traveled farther south along the coast, then east into the mountains. They saw falling stars and were quite impressed by them and they rebuilt a shrine together.

"We found an ancient foundation that must have been a very old shrine," Abi explained to us when they returned.

"It looked like it was the oldest shrine in the world!" interjected Kedar.

"The foundation was square, so we decided to rebuild it to make it as tall as it needed to be to form a cube," Abi continued. "Ishmael found an unusual rock and we didn't want to just leave it lying on the ground, so we put it in the cube. In all my years, I have never seen anything like that rock."

"What did it look like?"

"Ha! It was white until Kedar got his dirty hands all over it. It was black by the time we put it into the cube," Nebaioth teased.

"I did not turn it black!" Kedar gave his older brother a poke with his elbow.

"Did too!" Nebaioth said, poking him back.

"Did not!"

I had always thought that Ta-Sherit's eyelashes were the most expressive part of her eyes. But then I saw that a single lifted eyebrow could stop and silence two boisterous adolescents.

"Not so easy getting the roof up there," added Ishmael, laughing. "The cube was taller than any of us. So, Father climbed up on a big stone, then Yitzi gave me a leg up so I could climb onto Father's shoulders, and we got the job done."

"You are so heavy! I felt like my feet sank into that rock standing there with you weighing me down!" All five of them burst into laughter.

"There was also a cave," Abi said, turning serious. "There was a cave that I slept in one night during this trip, and there was something about it . . . I felt some kind of power. It wasn't a communication from El Shaddai, exactly, but there was power that night . . . "

"It's good to know that El Shaddai is present even that far from Canaan, and from Haran." I said.

"Is El Shaddai present everywhere? Or just where Grandfather Abraham is?" asked Nebaioth.

"I remember what you told me, Mama Sa-Sa," said Ta-Sherit "about King Melchizedek saying that El Shaddai was the maker of heaven and earth. So, it stands to reason that El Shaddai is present everywhere. And remember, Nebaioth, that the angel found me in the wilderness, twice, when Grandfather Abraham was not anywhere near."

"Ishmael," Abi addressed him seriously and suddenly, "Do not forget that cave. Find it again. Take your children and your children's children there, and pray to El Shaddai."

Chapter 27

I'M GLAD THE MEN had a good time, but from my point of view, their trip left me undistracted from my visit with Ta-Sherit, which originally had been the whole point of the trip. I was filled with joy and gratitude to El Shaddai that I had survived long enough to be able to accomplish my last goal and see her again.

Ta-Sherit was happily settled into her life as a matriarch. "Ish's wives do most of the work," she told me. "I deliver the babies and I have not lost one of them! You taught me well, Mama Sa-Sa. I still do the ritual of blessing my hands with hot water just before the baby comes out. Some people think it's silly, but I really do have good success when I perform the ritual. I love having all these babies and children to play with. I do the cuddling and playing while the mothers do the work. Good set-up, huh? We are not yet up to twelve sons, but we are getting there. Fourteen boys and girls. This family is a force to be reckoned with!"

"Each child is more adorable than the last. And your daughters-in-law seem suitable. Healthy and respectful. Do you get along with them?"

"Oh yes. They know who's in charge."

"And what about you? Has any man sought you in marriage?"

"Nah. Not for long, anyway. I don't need a man in my life. Any man comes sniffing around here, I tell him I'm an Egyptian princess and show him this gold necklace from Pharaoh. Thank you again, Mama Sa-Sa, it's been a very useful adornment to have, as well as being beautiful. They see the high-quality gold and fine Egyptian workmanship, and they know I'm out of their league. Or I tell them that I am already married to the richest, most important man in the land of Canaan, and they know they can't compete. I have all these grandchildren here to secure my future. And no one wants to mess with Ishmael. It's pretty clear no man can offer me anything I want that I don't already have."

"I'm delighted to see you with so many grandchildren. That one little boy seems particularly bright. What is his name?"

"Massa. Yes, he is smart. Wise, even, strange as it may seem to attribute wisdom to one who is still so young."

"Well, let's see if I can teach him something. Something I learned, eventually, about the right way to live, even though I must admit I have not done it often enough throughout my life."

"I want to hear this. Massa, come here and listen to Mama Sa-Sa."

I wondered how one of Ishmael's sons had come to have a name that sounds so much like Ta-Sherit's nickname for me. I'm glad I got the smart one, anyway.

"Here is a saying for you to remember, Massa: 'Speak up for those who have no voice, for the rights of those who are being crushed.' Perhaps you will grow up to be a wise teacher, my dear boy, and people will remember your words and your wisdom." I smiled at him and patted him on the head.

Massa thanked me politely, repeated the proverb I had just told him, and said he would remember that the poor have rights, even if they are not able to defend those rights themselves. Smart kid. May Holy One bless him and add to his wisdom.

"Hey, that's good," said Ta-Sherit. "Ishmael has a different attitude towards the poor. He says that the merciful thing to do is to let people who are in a bad situation drink as much beer and wine as they want so they can forget their misery and poverty. He himself does not drink much because he says he must keep a clear head and remember what he has said and what he needs to do. That's because he is successful, not poor and miserable. We have a good life here."

Our conversation roamed over many topics. I wanted to know what had happened when she and Ishmael were unable to find Lot, where they went, how they got here. Also, I'd noticed a scar on her arm that hadn't been there before.

"Oh! That is quite a story! Let me get you a drink first." Actually, it was one of Ishmael's wives who brought me the drink, when Ta-Sherit signaled her.

"When Ishmael and I realized we would not be able to find Cousin Lot, we decided to travel on to Egypt as planned anyway. Ishmael knew he was the one being sent away, and he asked me if I wanted to return to the house of Abraham, while he went on alone. Went on to what, I wondered. I was daunted by the prospect of what lay ahead of us, but I said I would go on with him. Eventually, we ran out of water. We were in the desert, no vegetation except for a couple of scraggly little trees, hardly more than bushes. Ishmael was about to collapse from thirst, so I put him in what little shade there was under one of the trees—there wasn't room for both of us. I still had enough energy to walk so I went a little farther away to try to find the last arrow Ishmael had shot—I think he had seen a mirage or a demon or something; there was nothing out there to shoot at—because I didn't want to waste the arrow when we had so little. Also, I couldn't stand to see my son like that and I was afraid he would die.

"I cried out to El Roi. And then, the angel of God spoke to me again! The God of hearing heard Ishmael and me! The angel told me not to be afraid and to lift Ishmael up and to make strong my hand in his. As I understood it, this meant more than just holding him tight with my hand—that would be simple—but that I, my hand, would be made strong if I stayed with him. I felt reassured that I had made the right choice back in the camp with you when I said I would go with my son, and again when I decided to stay with him when we couldn't find Cousin Lot, even though the journey turned out to be much harder than I'd expected. And the angel's words are indeed what came to pass: I have become stronger in so many ways by staying with Ishmael. And then you know what happened? Right after the angel spoke and I knew what I should do, the God who sees opened my eyes and what did I see? A well of water. God provides. Just what we needed, just when we needed it. A well of water in the desert! I filled the water skin, gave Ishmael a drink and when he was able, we moved on."

"I am so proud of you, Ta-Sherit. Twice, you have heard from an angel of Holy One. Twice, you have been saved from perishing in the wilderness. No one can deny that you are important to El Shaddai." I was also glad I had a cup of good cool water while listening to her story.

"We drank the water; our despair was dissolved by the water God provided. But we were still in the wilderness, with no destination and no direction. I prayed to God to show us a path. I got an answer—how can I say this? I heard an answer, but in my heart, not in my ears. 'The path does not yet exist. The path is made by walking.' Not exactly the kind of answer I was hoping for! But I came to see the wisdom and I came to see the challenge. I was going to make my own path, my own life, with my hand made strong in Ishmael's hand.

"It was a tough time for us, no doubt about it," she continued. "But even so, I feel like there was something different about me after that second rescue. I feel like I have been given some kind of a gift, or that my luck changed for the better since then, or some transformation took place in me. Wandering in the wilderness did something to us. The daily challenge of survival made us stronger. It was a hard time, for sure, but there was also something freeing about being in the wilderness. The feeling of freedom was surprising, but by then I was open to being surprised by God. It was just the two of us, depending on God and on each other, and because of that dependence, we were more aware of God's presence than we ever had been. I told Ishmael again about God, the one you call El Shaddai and that I call El Roi because of what happened to me. I told him again about the angel who came to me at Beer-lahai-roi the other time I wandered in the wilderness. And Ishmael understood. He finally understood! I know you and I and Abraham had told him about our God many times before, but he always shrugged it off. This second time, the angel also said that God had heard Ishmael's voice where he was. So, it wasn't just about me being heard. Ishmael understood that God had heard his voice, too, and he saw how God provided for us. We still had most of the silver you sewed into my robe, but you can't eat silver and it was a long time before we found a place to buy food. God provided us enough food and water, just enough, but enough to survive. We did not lack for anything that we really, truly needed. The wilderness can be a beautiful place."

She sighed and took a drink before she continued.

"When we entered Egypt, the Egyptians saw that I was very beautiful. We were stopped by two—I guess you would call them border guards— some kind of officials or soldiers of Pharaoh, anyway. They took one look at me and they decided I was coming with them and would be given to Pharaoh for his harem. For a moment I was amazed that I would go back to exactly where I came from. But the amazement did not last long; I had to stop this. I didn't think it was a good idea and I didn't want to do it. And what would happen to Ishmael?

"One Egyptian said, 'Let's kill her husband so she'll be an unmarried woman and there won't be any trouble.'

"No time to tell him he wasn't my husband. One of the Egyptian soldiers jumped Ishmael. They wrestled, and Ish just pounded the crap out of that guy. It did not take long. Meanwhile, the other one was dragging me away, while I struggled with him as best I could. We were at some distance and Ishmael shot an arrow. You remember how good an archer he was back in Canaan? He had become even better while hunting for our food in the desert. The Egyptian soldier was wearing armor and there wasn't much un-protected skin where Ishmael could land an arrow. Meanwhile, of course, I was right there, intertwined with the Egyptian. Ish put an arrow through the man's neck. Through it! What an aim! It ripped open that big vein in his neck, and blood gushed all over. He died quickly, but not before I could see the look of surprise on his stupid Egyptian face."

That "his hand against everyone" prophecy has its positive side, I thought to myself.

"It took me a moment to realize that the arrow tip had lodged in my upper arm, and that some of the blood on me was my own. After Ishmael was sure he had completely dispatched the first man, we got the arrow out, bound up my wound and hid the bodies in the sand. The wound didn't get infected, fortunately, but my skin healed kind of bumpy, as you see. And that was the end of our trip to Egypt. We turned around, kept moving and came down the east coast of the Red Sea. We settled here, across from Egypt but not in it."

I wondered if I should tell this story to Abraham.

"We settled here, and eventually our background became known, including that I am an expert midwife. And the story of the blessing of Ishmael spread through the land—that he would be the father of twelve princes, and they would become a great nation. Well, every family around here wants to get their daughter in on that! And of course, everyone is very impressed that I am a daughter of Pharaoh."

Good thing I never told her. But it crossed my mind to wonder if one of the Egyptian soldiers she and Ishmael dispatched was Ta-Sherit's father, Hakkin. That would be too big a coincidence. No. Don't think about it.

"So, I had my pick in choosing a wife for Ishmael. Or wives, I should say. One of them has died, unfortunately. But not in childbirth. And not postpartum—you are so right, Mama Sa-Sa. The first six weeks postpartum are so fragile; new mothers need a lot of care. She did not die due to anything related to childbirth. And my ability as a midwife is another reason families want their daughters to be married to Ishmael. He has three wives now, I run this household and El Roi has seen us and blessed us with prosperity."

There is not much more to say about our visit and our trip back to Canaan. Ta-Sherit and I talked about everything we had to talk about. The men came back from their adventure and in due course we packed up for our return journey. Isaac asked his father if he could stay and live with Ishmael, but Abi was adamant that he must not. "The whole point was to get to Canaan. That is where you need to be, in your own space. We are not sure what this covenant is all about, but it is for you and your descendants. You are not part of your brother's household. It is important for you to stay in Canaan." Isaac took his father's words so seriously that I would not be surprised if he never left the land of Canaan again.

It was hard saying goodbye to my girl. I told her, just as I had told her so many times before, that she had been a beautiful baby. "Not your first baby. But your first child," she said, smiling. And I smiled, too.

I would like to say that we had left nothing unsaid between us during this last visit but that is not quite true. For example, as I just said, I never told her about her real father and I don't regret it. I wonder what she never told me that I will never know. There must have been a great deal that happened between her finding water in the wilderness of Beer-sheba when she and Ishmael were about to die of thirst, and when the two of them set up this successful trading business and thriving family. There is quite a bit about my life in the harem that no one but me knows. I never told Abi about my first pregnancy and how I ended it; I still think that was the right decision. I wonder what he never told me about his life in Egypt when we were separated. But it doesn't matter, we have gotten to where we are and that is good enough.

On our trip back, we again stopped at the spring of Beer-lahai-roi and watered the animals. Abraham was soon ready to move on with his servants and get back to his people and his flocks at Beer-sheba but Isaac wanted to stay a few days longer. I know he was hoping for a visitation or a message from Holy One, and I didn't want to say no to him. Maybe it would happen for him. As for me, I did not think that Holy One had anything further to say to me. Except, perhaps, "Welcome home."

And so, Beer-lahai-roi, the well of the Living One Who Sees Me, is the last place I saw Abraham, son of Terah, son of Nahor, son of Serug, and said goodbye to him. Abraham, the man who made my life what it was, the other tree who grew from the same root as I did. I don't know if he knew that this would be our last goodbye, but I was certain of it.

Isaac and I, with our servants, proceeded on to Hebron, my beloved Hebron. Isaac helped me pitch my tent by Mamre's oaks, my favorite trees in all the world. I used to be able to do that by myself. How many times in my life have I pitched a tent? I was feeling every one of my years as I lay down in my blankets in my tent. I felt that I had rotted and dried up. I had been born in Ur a long time ago and I would die here in Hebron. Soon. It has been a long time since I've played senet net hab, the game of passing through, that I learned in Egypt. But now I know that I have moved all my pieces to the end of the board.

I prayed, "Holy One, now you can dismiss your servant in peace because you have kept your promise. My eyes have seen everything that they need to see. Holy One, show your glory to all my family who know you, and reveal your bright light to all who are not my family."

Afterward

Chapter 28

Isaac here. My mother died in her tent at Hebron, with me and my father holding her hands and many of our people gathered around. When she was fading, she called out for her sister Merai, and for someone whose name I didn't recognize; it sounded like Deedee. I thought it curious that she also called out for Terah. It's strange that he was on her mind, even though I knew she'd always had great respect for my grandfather.

When I could see that the end was near, I had sent word to my father; I really couldn't not tell him. He came immediately. Father was hit hard by her death. I've never seen him weep like that. He retold that old story of his dream about the palm tree and the cedar tree. "And now, the cedar tree stands alone," he wailed. It looked to me like he shrank, physically, during his mourning.

The next thing to be done was to locate a suitable burial place. We didn't own one; we didn't own any land. My father had a particular piece of land in mind that he hoped to buy, and he wanted me to come along while he negotiated its purchase from the Heth clan; one of its members owned the land. I was interested to see how this would go, but I asked Damascan Eliezer to come, too, even though it wasn't far. It was a complicated negotiation. First, Father told all the members of the Heth clan who were sitting at their village gate that he wanted to buy the cave of Machpelah, which was owned by Ephron Ben Zohar. Fortunately, Ephron was one of the men there at the time. He offered it to Father as a gift, which at first one would think was great luck and a bargain. Ephron said this about giving it as a gift in the presence of his people, so there were plenty of witnesses to it being a gift. But Father insisted on paying for it. That Ephron was a sly one. He said the piece of land—a field with a cave at the end of it—was worth four hundred shekels and he made it sound as if that was a mere pittance. I was astonished that Father agreed to such a price, with no bargaining. Father weighed out the silver he had brought along, right then and there, making sure everyone present saw that it was done properly. Four hundred shekels. An outrageously high price for that piece of land. Especially when he could have had it as a gift. Maybe it was Father's way of showing that he cared. Maybe it showed that he was too grief-stricken to think clearly.

I watched but did not say anything. I figured that Father wanted me, a younger man who would likely outlive him, Eliezer, and most of these Heth men, to be there so I could testify to the details of the transaction if any of the Heth clan tried to reclaim ownership of the property after the death of Ephron Ben Zohar. Once we were back at our tents in Hebron, Eliezer explained to me why Father did it this way. By paying, he obtained better title to the land than he would have if the land were a gift. Also, paying the whole price that was originally requested prevents anyone from saying that Father tricked Ephron Ben Zohar into a bad deal. He also explained that owning burial land was an important factor that our family could use to support our claim to legal residence. Eliezer knows about that kind of thing.

All these years, we had been sojourners, moving from place to place, even though there were places we returned to regularly. That seemed to be good enough. We had accumulated wealth in other forms, but we did not own land. Of course, from time to time some of our household died and we buried them, but we just buried them where we were and did not have a formal burial place that we owned. Now that Mother had died, Father suddenly was motivated to attend to certain matters. Surely, he was thinking about his own mortality and how much time he had left to do whatever else he needed to do in his life.

Mother's passing hit me hardest when Father and I prepared her body. I wish Ta-Sherit had been there with us. We wrapped her in the finest Egyptian linen we had. Mother always liked linen. I had heard about her time in Egypt and knew that she had acquired a taste for wearing linen while she was there. Even though she took a dim view of most aspects of Egyptian culture, she did like their linen. I considered also wrapping her in an old wool blanket that she was fond of. It was an odd size, and the pattern was all wrong and asymmetrical. She had used it as a baby blanket for me because it was too small for normal use. You could see that it had been woven with fine quality wool, but it was so old it was in pretty bad condition. It might seem disrespectful to bury her with such a crummy old thing, even if she did like it, so I didn't even suggest it to Father. Maybe if I put it under my pillow, I will dream of her.

We carried her to what used to be called the cave of Machpelah, and buried her facing those oaks of Mamre she loved so much. At the last minute, I ran to the nearest tree and broke off a small branch of oak to tuck inside her wrappings. As I did so, it occurred to me that this tree was now my family's tree. It was clear both to Father and me, without anything being said, that I would bury him there someday. Another unspoken expectation was that I, too, would be buried there. And then what? Who else will be buried there? Will our family be forgotten?

We decided on Mother's age as one hundred and twenty-seven years.

On the way back from laying her in the cave, I asked Father how he had chosen that cave as our family's burial place. "You seemed intent on buying this piece of land, this one and no other, and getting good title to it," I said. I refrained from saying anything about burial being so much better than being set on fire on top of a mountain.

"I discovered this cave a long time ago," he sighed. "Do you remember what I told you about the visit from the three strangers who told your mother and me that she would conceive and give birth to you?" I nodded. I'd heard it many times. I would inherit an everlasting covenant, whatever that meant. "I was so eager to show hospitality to these visitors, even before I knew what they were there to tell us. I told your mother to bake a huge amount of bread for them, and I, myself, ran to the herd to select the best calf to serve to them. I knew which one I wanted, and when I chased it, it ran into what was called the cave of Machpelah. I followed it in and caught it, but while I was there, I felt something. It was not the overwhelming feeling of the presence of El Shaddai, but it was a similar feeling on a smaller scale, something special about the presence of the place. And I knew then that this was the place I wanted as our family's burial cave."

"That was a long time ago." A long time between decision and action, I thought. I wonder if he thought he had all the time in the world, and that he and Mother would never die.

Chapter 29

FATHER'S NEXT PROJECT WAS to find a wife for me. I had been of marriageable age for quite a while, and suddenly Father realized I'm supposed to have a family, too. When we visited Ta-Sherit, I knew that Mother was tactfully observing Ishmael's daughters to see if any of them would be suitable for me, but Father forbade my marrying any of them. Just like he forbade me from settling there to live with Ishmael.

When we were travelling north after visiting Ta-Sherit and Ishmael, we ran into a band of traders coming south, who had recently dealt with Father's brother Nahor, all the way back in Haran. The traders told Father all about the eight sons Nahor's wife, Milcah, had borne to him, and about the other four sons he had by his concubine Reumah. Naturally, Nahor had a lot of daughters and granddaughters, too. This encounter with the traders put the idea in Father's heart that he should look for a wife for me among his Haran relatives, specifically, Nahor's family.

But Father was not going to go there himself. His plan was to send Damascan Eliezer, making it very clear that Eliezer was not to take me there with him to meet any of the women myself. It's kind of funny how Father had such an attachment to his relatives there, most of whom were young enough that he'd never met them, and at the same time, he also had an attachment to the land of Canaan, where none of them live. "They were supposed to be here," he insisted. "But only Lot would come. Coming here was the whole point. God said he would show me the land where we should be, and here I am. I am not going back, and you should not go back there, either." The command to leave Haran and go to another land was the first instruction Father received from El Shaddai, and it still had a hold on him. I had heard many times how overwhelming the power of El

Shaddai felt. I wonder if I will hear from El Shaddai again. Maybe when Father, too, has passed on?

Damascan Eliezer was a servant, but you wouldn't know it to look at him. He was always well-dressed and had a formal, authoritative way about him. Father trusted him completely. He was Father's oldest servant and they had been through so much together, both good times and bad. Mother, too, respected his ability as a manager, but I sensed some disappointment or distance on her part regarding him. She never said anything against him, though, so I don't know if there was a problem or if so, what it was. I liked him well enough, and he was always respectful to me.

Eliezer, not Mother or Father, was the one who would find a wife for me. Finding me a wife was important to me! Eliezer and Father had a conversation about it, but I was not included in it. Later, I caught up with Eliezer and told him what I wanted. He said he would do his best to find the right woman, that he would pray to Father's God for a sign as to who was the right woman. Mostly, Eliezer was concerned that the woman might not be willing to come back with him to Canaan. If not, I could be out of luck. Or rather, Father would be out of luck as I would marry a Canaanite woman instead of one of his relatives. Eliezer is taking some heavy gold jewelry with him as a gift, so we hope that will get the point across that I am not just some poor shepherd.

I hope Eliezer finds the right woman. I want, more than anything else, to be happily married with just one wife. I don't want a bunch of wives and concubines, even though when I inherit, I will be wealthy enough for all that. Peace. Lots of children and everyone getting along with each other. No family strife. That is what I want in my life. "One is enough," my mother told me during her final weeks. So, I think that goes for me, too, regarding marriage.

Shortly before he left for Haran, Eliezer came to talk to me about Mother. "Your mother was a remarkable woman, Master Isaac. For many years, I, like many other people, only thought of her as Master Abraham's beautiful but barren wife. But anyone who knows only that she was beautiful has merely the shallowest understanding of her. She knew more about midwifery than any other woman I have ever known. Her knowledge and skill were truly important contributions to the prosperity of the house of Abraham. She lost fewer babies and mothers than most midwives do. Of course, there are always some who cannot be saved, but it is a real loss of resources when you lose a mother or baby in childbirth. She and I used to argue about how much work newly-delivered mothers should do, and how long they should rest. I am in charge of work assignments, but she was insistent that new mothers need a good long recovery period. Eventually, I came to see she was right. She was also right about her insistence that pregnant women drink plenty of milk and water. It took me years to be convinced, but I came to see a difference in strength and health between the servants born in our house as opposed to those we acquired from elsewhere. She was truly a woman of wisdom. Whatever advice she gave you throughout your life, Master Isaac, you should remember it."

I thanked him. That night in bed, I wept, realizing how much I had lost.

The next morning, he found me and had a little more to say. "Another thing about your mother, Master Isaac. She was quite remarkable in her care of that girl Ta-Sherit whom she brought with her from the house of Pharaoh. Mistress Sarah had no obligation to her and yet she treated her like a daughter—even though it was obvious that Ta-Sherit the Egyptian was not Master Abraham's daughter. Most people would put a fatherless foreign girl like that to work and forget about her. Your mother had a mind of her own about raising her and training her to be a midwife. They were quite a pair, those two. The loyalty your mother showed, raising the Egyptian girl so attentively like that . . . well, it's admirable."

I thanked him again and wished him well on his journey.

"It will be difficult to find a woman as beautiful as your mother, let alone one with all her other virtues. But I have prayed and will continue to pray, that the God of Master Abraham, Mistress Sarah and Master Isaac will lead me to the right wife for you."

Curious that he speaks of the God of my parents and me, but not as his God. Yet he's willing to pray to that God. I wonder what he believes.

Chapter 30

WHEN MY MOTHER'S END was near, I sent word not only to Father but also to Ta-Sherit. She lived so far away that I knew there was no way she could arrive in time to be with Mother in her final days. She did come, though, many weeks later, when Damascan Eliezer was on his trip to Father's relatives in Haran.

She came with her two oldest grandsons, Nebaioth and Kedar. Of course, the two of them remembered me from our adventure with Father and Ishmael, and it cheered me up a bit to see them again. It was a little awkward that I did not have a wife or sister to entertain a female guest. So, I spent a lot of time attending to Ta-Sherit during her visit. Even though my three visitors were quite different from the mysterious three visitors whom I had heard about so often, my parents had impressed upon me the importance of hospitality. Ta-Sherit had been important to Mother, so that meant she was important to me. Also, she seemed to have an aura of spirituality and wisdom about her that intrigued and attracted me.

"In her last days, Mother told me there was something I was to give to you." I brought out an old money bag, which I had never seen until Mother told me where to find it among her belongings. It was empty, but it was a large, nice-looking bag, decorated with intricate needlework in a style used by some tribes in the Negev.

It took a moment for a look of recognition to come across Ta-Sherit's face, but then she shook her head, with a sad smile and tears ran down her face as she took it.

"I'm sorry it's empty," I said. "That's how it was when I found it."

"Oh, that's not why I'm crying," she said, before she burst out laughing. "I'm amazed that she kept it all this time."

I didn't know what to make of this crying and laughing, but it does seem that mourning brings out a strange combination of feelings. I guess she knows something I don't about the money bag.

Nebaioth and Kedar were interested in how we cared for our flocks and herds. Our way of life and the terrain that made it possible were different from what they were used to. So, they were content to spend their days with some of the herdsmen who were about their age. They had met Mother on our recent visit, but since they had spent most of that time with me and Father and Ishmael, one could not expect a lot of mourning and reminiscing from them beyond the usual formalities.

I was a little disappointed that Ishmael did not come, too. "He started out with us," Ta-Sherit assured me, "but we stopped at your father's camp at Beer-sheba on the way and he wanted Ishmael to stay with him a while. So, he may come later. Ishmael will come to help you bury your father when the time comes. I will make sure of that. But I don't think that's going to happen anytime soon."

"I wonder if Father is trying to keep us apart. He was insistent that I should not live with Ishmael's family."

"Well . . . Ishmael has a strong personality and maybe Abraham is concerned that he will trick you out of your birthright or something like that."

"It is true that I am much quieter than he is. But so long as I have eyes to see, no one is going to trick me out of my birthright or my place in the covenant." I paused. "How is Father?"

"He's well. He's given to long periods of silence. But I guess he always was like that. You must have met the young woman named Keturah when you visited his camp in Beer-sheba when you and Mama Sa-Sa were on the way to visit me? I think you're going to have some more half-siblings, Yitzi," she smiled.

"What? So soon?"

"Wives mourn; husbands replace." She shrugged. "Keturah is strong and healthy. I spent some time in their camp on my way here. I think she's happy with the idea that she will be the wife of a prominent man like Abraham. But when your father isn't in a silent mood, he usually talks about Sarah, compares Sarah favorably to all other women, including Keturah. It would be hard for any woman to live up to the legend that Sarah is becoming in your father's memory. The only thing the girl can do to distinguish herself is to have lots of sons for Abraham. So, I think that is exactly what she hopes to do. She sure didn't want him wasting any seed on me, which was fine by me. She had me stay in her tent, even though I am still married to Abraham. She was very hospitable and all, but I think she wanted to keep an eye on me. Ha! Well, Keturah's young. She already has a name picked out for her first son: Jokshan."

"Hmmm. Doesn't Father have something to say about names?"

"I would think so. Come to think of it, both you and Ishmael had your names assigned by God. So maybe Abraham will want to have his turn to choose. I am quite sure he will want to name the first girl after the legendary Sarah. I would not be surprised if he names all of the girls Sarah or Sarai or Sa-Sa."

"Maybe you, too, will become legendary. The brilliant, beautiful, expert midwife Ta-Sherit. Daughter of a Pharaoh. Raised as a daughter by the great and beautiful Sarah. Milk-sister of Isaac, yet also his step-mother. Second wife of Abraham. Mother of Ishmael and grandmother of twelve princes. I think you provide plenty of good material for future generations to craft into an amazing legend."

"It depends on who tells the story." She shook her head ruefully. "What they remember, what they leave out. And what they embellish beyond recognition."

"Yes. Like the story of Father rescuing Cousin Lot from King Chedorlaomer and the other great kings. How many were there, again?" We laughed together and I felt grateful for our easy comradery. It was a comfort to be with someone who knows my parents and knows my family stories even though I don't know her very well. I miss my mother. Ta-Sherit helps fill the emptiness.

"But what about you? I am surprised you are not married yet," she asked gently.

"I hope I will be soon," I smiled. "Father sent Damascan Eliezer back to Haran to look for a wife for me among the family of his brother Nahor. He does not want me to marry a Canaanite woman; he is quite definite about that."

"Your mother made all the difference in my life. I still feel her love every day," Ta-Sherit said quietly when we went to visit the burial cave. "She picked me up and shaped me like a potter shapes clay. If I had stayed with my birth mother in the house of Pharaoh, my life would have had no purpose, like clay that stays in the ground. Your mother could have shaped me into any kind of a woman. She could have let me grow up to be just another one of the ordinary workers, married to some other one of the ordinary workers, mother of ordinary children, assuming they survived. Instead, she taught me her midwifery skill and I became an expert. She taught me about El Shaddai—although it took me a long time to understand what she and Abraham had experienced and were talking about. If I had stayed in Egypt, I would have worshipped a long line-up of Egyptian gods and goddesses and would never have known El Shaddai. Instead, I have experienced visitations, twice. An angel has rescued me twice and I know that I matter to Holy One. So much better than keeping track of the mindless duties owed to a bunch of silent, unhearing, and unseeing figurines. Like Khonsu. When I was young, I thought Khonsu was important. Can you believe it?" she said shaking her head.

"I was rescued, too. The angel spoke to Father, not me, though. I hope I, too, will be blessed with another visitation. That feeling . . . I want to feel it again." I'm a little envious of Ta-Sherit's visitation experiences. I decided right then that I would move to Beer-lahai-roi as soon as I could after marrying.

"Your mother rescued me, too. She rescued me at birth. Once when we were delivering a baby who had his umbilical cord wrapped around his neck, she told me about my own birth. She didn't speak of it in terms of her rescuing me, but now that I know more about that sort of thing, yes, that's what happened. I wonder if she rescued me even before my birth, if she did something to help my birth mother carry me to full term and not miscarry. She knew a lot about pregnancy care as well as about childbirth. I guess I will never know now."

After thinking about it, she continued, "She rescued me in a different way by getting me out of the house of Pharaoh. My life might have been easier and maybe even luxurious if I had stayed there, but it would have been so empty and pointless. Marrying your father was also a kind of a rescue for me."

I don't know about that, but if she's glad of it, then so am I. "I wonder if the wife Eliezer brings back for me will feel like she is being rescued by joining our family."

"Yes, she will. Her life will have purpose and she will be remembered because of her role in the family of Abraham."

"You seem to know a lot about the future," I smiled. "I don't even know for sure if Damascan Eliezer is going to come back from Haran with anyone. He was concerned that he might find the right woman but she would be unwilling to come back here with him."

"Ummm." She paused. "Yeah." Another pause. "I don't like to talk about it, but . . . ever since the second time when Holy One rescued me in the wilderness, I seem to have been blessed with some kind of a gift about seeing the future. Sometimes. It's hard to explain."

"Tell me what you can."

"Well, anyone who sees Abraham and Keturah together does not need to be a fortune teller to guess that he is going to marry her. And if I could foresee exactly what is about to happen and when, I would be out in the desert betting on camel races. So, it's not like that. But sometimes I know things no human being has ever told me. I don't claim to be able to speak for Holy One. All I can say is, sometimes I just . . . know things about the future. Look, Ishmael and I were about to die in the desert. A couple years later, we were established near a trading route with a prosperous business. What happened in between? I had a few good insights about what to do, how best to use the silver your mother had given me, who to trust, who not to trust. Sometimes it comes to me in dreams; sometimes it just comes to me."

I did not know about Mother giving her silver, but was pleased to hear it.

"So, yes, you will marry a woman from the Haran relatives, you will have sons. Abraham will have more sons, maybe half a dozen more. He will send them away from the land of Canaan, just like he sent Ishmael away to the south beyond Canaan."

I wonder if she's right. El Shaddai did promise Father a large family.

She sighed, picked up my hand, and continued. "I wish I could tell you a way to ensure that all the sons and daughters of Abraham could prosper, worship Holy One, and live peacefully together. I know that is what he wants, and what Sarah and I want."

Acknowledgments

I AM GRATEFUL TO the many people whose support turned my daydream into a book.

The team at Wipf and Stock, including Matt Wimer, Joe Delahanty, Calvin Jaffarian, and copyeditor Caleb Kormann.

The Wesley Theological Seminary community provided the seed bed (the literal meaning of "seminary") in which this project grew. Dr. Bruce Birch taught my first class in Hebrew Bible, and Dr. Denise Dombkowski Hopkins taught me the Hebrew language, some of which I still remember. In due course, I was honored to work with each of them as a teaching assistant for their "Introduction to Hebrew Bible" classes. Working with Denise resulted in my marinating in the text for twelve years. I gained further understanding as I journeyed through the Hebrew Bible on slightly different paths as the teaching assistant for other professors: Dr. Paul Cho, Dr. Amy Beth Jones, and Dr. David Hopkins. Thanks also to Claudia Barnes, who taught the first class I took at Wesley, New Testament Greek. If her class had not been such a wonderful and welcoming experience, none of the above would have happened. In addition to the professors at Wesley, thanks are due to the many other scholars whose books, articles, lectures, sermons, and videos I was exposed to over the years as a student and as a teaching assistant and that informed my research for this book. I'll just note two: *Womanist Midrash* by Wilda Gafney and *Women's Bible Commentary*, edited by Carol Newsom, Sharon Ringe, and Jacqueline Lapsley.

This is a better book because of the input, feedback, and insights of early readers and editors: Kathryn Johnson, Dr. Denise Dombkowski Hopkins, Rena Margulis, Abby Dailey, Louise Strait, Dr. Paul Cho, Jan Moody, Rev. Susan Graceson, Dr. Meg Baker, and Kathleen Henderson Staudt.

I am also grateful for the encouragement of many people who supported this project and helped me learn about the publishing industry. Special thanks go to Walter Stahr, who provided much help, inspiration, and encouragement.

The Writer's Center in Bethesda, Maryland, provided helpful workshops and sometimes magical events.

My beloved husband, Paul, with whom I'm blessed to share my life, supported me in so many ways throughout this project.

And greatest thanks to God, from whom all blessings flow.

Printed in Great Britain
by Amazon

59064310R00096